Sapphire Stone Adventures of Pirate Captain Skye

by

Lene Moller

Pirate Captain Skye Adventures Sapphire Stone

By: Lene Moller

Dedication

I dedicate this book to several people who helped and supported me. To my nephew, Connor, who told me not to worry about my grammar and supported me all the way to the finish. To my daughter-in-law, Jessica, who listened to all my different storylines. To my son, Keaton, who was brutally honest with me when he read my book and also encouraged me to start the next book in the series. To my sister, Dianette, who read my rough drafts and gave encouraging feedback. Last but not least, to two of my grandchildren, Avery (Queen Ava in the book) and Kalieanne (Princess Kalieanna), both of whom love hearing my pirate stories.

Preface

There was a young ten-year-old orphan named Gabe who lived in Fredens Land. His parents were merchants who were killed on their way to Onsedale. He lived in the orphanage with his sister Katie. Gabe was an intelligent young boy, very aware of his surroundings. Lately, he had started to notice that orphans were disappearing in the middle of the night. They would be there at bedtime, then in the morning, be gone. When Gabe asked the Headmaster about it, he was told they were adopted.

Gabe tried to ask more questions but was told to mind his business. Tomorrow, his friend Princess Kalieanna was coming for her weekly visit. She would come each week to see how the orphans were doing. Sometimes they would play pirates with sticks they found. The next day, Gabe anxiously waited for Princess Kalieanna to arrive. Princess Kalieanna finally came and gave each one of them a hug. Gabe said he needed to discuss something very important with her. She asked, "What is it?" Gabe replied, "Not here. Let's go outside so we won't be overheard." Gabe explained to Kalieanna that everyone would be there at bed check, but in the morning, one or two of the children would be missing. Kalieanna asked, "Did you ask the Headmaster about it?" Gabe said, "Yes, he said they were adopted." Kalieanna replied, "That is strange. Why would they be getting adopted in the middle of the night?" Gabe told her, "I am scared that I could be next, and then who would look out for Katie?" Kalieanna came up with a plan. "I will sneak down here after my parents go to sleep and investigate what is going on. I will then report it to my father, King Jakob." Kalieanna said she needed to go home and have dinner with her family to avoid raising any suspicion. They said their goodbyes. Kalieanna made her way back to the castle and went up to her room to change out of her dirty clothes. She cleaned up and made it to her parents' room for dinner. After dinner, she went back to her room to wait. Her mother, the queen, came to check on her and tuck her in. Her mother finally left, and Kalieanna changed into some rags so she would blend in at the orphanage. She waited until her parents were asleep. She snuck down the hall and headed toward the kitchen, planning to leave through the servants' entrance. She was almost to the door when she heard a voice that scared her to death. Her sister Ava was standing there, asking, "Where do you think you're going in the middle of the night? And why are you dressed like a peasant?" Kalieanna explained that she needed to go to the orphanage to help Gabe and Katie. Ava asked, "What could you possibly help them with in the middle of the night?" Kalieanna said, "I'd rather not say until I have more proof." Ava said, "You should tell Father. He can help." Kalieanna said, "Not yet," and told Ava, "I will be back very quickly, I promise." Reluctantly, Ava let her go, gave her a hug, and said good night.

Kalieanna made her way down to the orphanage. She went through the kitchen entrance to meet with Gabe and Katie. At first, she didn't see them. They came out of their hiding spots in the pantry. Katie pointed to Kalieanna's outfit and giggled, "You look like a boy." Gabe looked at her and said, "With that cap on your head covering your hair, you really do." Kalieanna asked if anything was happening. Gabe said, "Yes, we heard two men talking to the Headmaster."

Kalieanna wanted to get a better look, so she climbed up the kitchen cabinet. From there, she could see the two men holding large duffel bags and talking to the Headmaster. She was trying to hear what they were saying, but she lost her balance and fell to the floor with a loud bang.

Gabe rushed over to her to see if she was okay and told Katie to go and hide. The two men burst into the kitchen. Gabe tried to defend them, but they were too big. The men grabbed Gabe and Kalieanna, tied their hands and feet, and stuffed socks into their mouths. Then they were put into the duffel bags. They were carried down to the shore and thrown into a rowboat. They rowed out to a big ship. They were carried down some stairs and then thrown into the hull at the bottom of the ship.

They were tossed out of the duffel bags and told this was their home for the next few days. When the men left, they untied each other and checked out their surroundings. It was dark and stinky. Kalieanna told Gabe not to worry, her father would surely send out a search party. Gabe said, "Hopefully, he sends the fleet." They were down in the hull for days; they would sleep, play games, and eat the stale bread they were fed. Finally, they docked. One of the crew members came down and told them to go up on deck. They made their way up to the deck. The sun was bright since they hadn't seen the sun in days. Gabe looked around and noticed a group of children—all boys ages 7 to 12. He pointed to Kalieanna and said, "They are all boys; you need to pretend to be a boy." Gabe fixed her hat to make sure no hair was coming out. The crew member told them to go over with the other children. They made their way over to the group. Gabe was trying to figure out what was going on. Then, to his horror, he realized it was an auction block, and the children were being bid on. The children were being pushed out onto the platform, and pirate captains would bid on them.

Finally, it was Gabe's turn. He fetched a good price, being so big for his age. Next, Kalieanna was put on the block. She looked so tiny, Gabe thought. Kalieanna wasn't getting any bids. Gabe shouted at her to think—Kal knew she hated that nickname. Kalieanna looked around her surroundings and saw one of the henchmen was not paying attention. Kalieanna grabbed his sword—she was an excellent swordsman, her father had taught her. She held out the sword as the henchman tried to get it back. He had no luck. Then his friend tried to help. Kalieanna decided to have some fun—she took her sword and cut both men's belts. Their pants fell to the ground, and there were roars of laughter from the audience. Then, out of the crowd, there was a booming voice yelling, "STOP." The crowd was silent. "I will pay 10 coins for the scrappy little boy." Kalieanna was bought by Captain Skeleton of the Red Hawk. Gabe was bought by Captain Kidd of the Revenge. They were going their separate ways—Gabe was going to the Revenge, and Kalieanna was going to the Red Hawk. Gabe and Kalieanna hugged one last time before they were torn apart. As Kalieanna was walking away, Gabe felt very guilty. He should have never gotten her involved in all of this—it was all his fault. As Gabe was being ushered away, he caught a glimpse of Kalieanna. It would be the last time he saw her.

Gabe was taken aboard the Revenge, where he was forced to cater to the captain's every need. If he spoke out or didn't follow orders, he was flogged. Gabe learned to just do his duties. The crew was starting to trust him. He was getting more freedom to move about the ship, but deep down, he was always planning his escape. He stayed in hopes that they would run into the Red Hawk, where Kalieanna had been taken hostage.

It had been two years, and he hadn't heard anything. They were making their way to Pirate's Cove to get supplies. Gabe hoped there would be news of the Red Hawk. They docked. Gabe was in the captain's quarters cleaning when the first officer rushed in. He said, "Captain, I have some news." Captain Kidd said, "Spit it out, then." "It's about the Red Hawk." Gabe's ears perked up. "The Red Hawk was in the Caribbean when a horrible storm came out of nowhere and destroyed the ship; there were no survivors." Gabe gasped. "Is there a problem, boy?" asked the captain. Gabe said, "No," and went on cleaning. Gabe hurried to finish so he could leave the cabin. Gabe realized Kalieanna was dead, and there was no more reason to keep searching for her. He had to get off the ship and return home to tell the King and Queen.

Gabe had been planning his escape for a long time. He waited until most of the crew left the ship, with only a few staying back to watch it. They soon would be drunk and passed out. Gabe made his way to the captain's quarters and found the gold watch he was looking for—that would buy his passage home. Gabe left the ship and found a merchant ship headed to Fredens Land. He gave the gold watch as payment.

Gabe stood on the bow of the ship, wondering how he was going to tell Kalieanna's parents that she was dead and it was all his fault.

----

15 years later

15 years had passed, but the memory of his lost friend still haunted Captain Gabriel Wateman. Standing tall at 6 foot 5 inches, with jet black hair and piercing sapphire blue eyes, he commanded the Queen's Navy with strength and confidence. His muscular physique was evident even under his crisp red Naval uniform. Women couldn't help but be drawn to him, but Gabe had no interest in romance. He had a duty to fulfill - to find and execute pirates under his queen's orders.

As one of the most feared and ruthless captains, Gabe showed no mercy to any pirate who crossed his path. This was fueled by a personal vendetta - many years ago, pirates had taken his dear friend Princess Kalianna captive. When he learned that her ship had sunk and there were no survivors, he managed to escape and eventually returned home to his kingdom. He informed his king and queen of their daughter's tragic fate, devastating them both. The queen fell into a deep depression while the king sought revenge by building ships and creating a massive naval barricade.

Gabe wasted no time in joining the Navy and quickly rose through the ranks until he became captain. He was now commissioned by Queen Ava, Kalianne's sister. As they sailed on their latest mission, they successfully destroyed Captain Blackbeard's ship and claimed their booty. Blackbeard and his crew were taken into custody, while their leader met his end as his ship sank.

Amongst the treasures they retrieved was a beautiful spyglass with intricate symbols etched onto it. When fully stretched out, it measured about two feet long. Gabe couldn't help but be intrigued by these mysterious codes, wondering what secrets they held. The symbols etched on it were like a secret code, begging to be deciphered. But for now, it was safely stashed away in his cabin.

Captain Gabriel and his crew were sailing towards Pirates Cove, their destination set on capturing the elusive pirate captain known as Skye. Rumors circulated that she was there, restocking her supplies. Gabriel had been chasing her for years, always one step behind. He couldn't help but wonder if someone on his own ship was leaking information to her. After all, what were a few gold coins to some men?

But this time, he had a reliable source - one of Skye's own crew members had betrayed her and told Gabriel's first officer of her whereabouts. They would arrive in just a day's time. Gabriel could practically taste victory and the large bounty that came with capturing Skye.

Her reputation preceded her - she was ruthless, showing no mercy to any who crossed her path. Men feared her and yet still followed her blindly. But Gabriel was determined to finally capture the most wanted pirate and claim the reward for himself. Perhaps then he could retire and buy land and a comfortable home for himself.

The thought of finally catching Skye sent a surge of adrenaline through Gabriel's veins as he eagerly awaited their arrival at Pirates Cove.

Captain Gabriel stood at the helm of his ship, scanning the horizon with a determined gaze. His crew bustled around him, preparing for their voyage to Pirates Cove. Rumors had been circulating that the elusive Captain Skye was there, stocking up. They would arrive at Pirates Cove in just one day. Gabriel felt a surge of excitement - finally, he would catch the most wanted pirate in the seven seas. The bounty on her head was enough to buy him a comfortable life on land - perhaps even a wife and children.

But as he thought about settling down, a small part of him still longed for the thrill of the open sea and the rush of a daring adventure. Could he really leave it all behind for a quiet life? Only time would tell. But first, he needed to catch Captain Skye and claim his prize.

Meanwhile:

Captain Skye stood proudly at the helm of her ship, the Vixen. The sturdy wooden vessel had once belonged to her father before he passed away, and she had taken over his legacy with determination and skill. Her long golden hair billowed in the wind as they set sail, and men couldn't help but stare at her beauty. Her eyes were a striking shade of Caribbean blue, and many said they could get lost in them forever.

Standing tall at five feet ten inches, Skye commanded attention with her presence alone. She wore black pants and a blouse, with a blue bandana tied around her forehead. Despite her captain attire, her curves were still evident and it was clear that she was not someone to be underestimated. A sash hung around her waist, holding the sword that her father had given her - a symbol of her authority.

Her crew respected and feared her; she had earned their loyalty through hard work and fierce determination. As a child, she grew up among the crew while her father was captain, and they had known her all her life. At just seven years old, she had learned how to defend herself, and by ten, she had made her first kill. Over the years, her heart had hardened, and she showed no mercy for mutiny or dishonesty. The rumors about her were wild - some said she was created by Satan himself, with fire running through her veins.

Despite her fearsome reputation, Skye's crew would follow her anywhere. And recently, she had tasked them with finding something very valuable - the legendary sapphire stone. This precious gem was said to grant any desire to its owner, making it a highly sought-after treasure among pirates.

Skye's father had once possessed a map that would lead them to the sapphire stone, but it was stolen by Captain Blackbeard. Before he passed away, he made Skye promise to find the map and the stone. And now, they were on their way to Pirate's Cove, where they knew Captain Gabriel was headed. Skye had a spy planted on his ship, and they were setting a trap to kidnap him and hold him for ransom.

As they sailed towards their destination, Skye couldn't help but think back to her father's deathbed and his final wish for her. She was determined to fulfill his vow and find the sapphire stone, no matter what it took. Her lack of emotions and love for others were replaced with an insatiable greed and desire for material wealth, making her overconfident in her pursuit. But as long as her crew stood by her side, she knew that nothing could stop them from achieving their goal. They would arrive at Pirate's Cove shortly. Skye made her way down to her cabin to change into an evening dress appropriate for her random meeting with Captain Gabriel. Her quarters were quite big. It had a bedroom, a beautiful library with books from around the world, and a beautiful hand-carved oak desk that her father got in Spain. She made her way into her bedroom. Skye unhooked the silver buckles of her pirate clothes. She opened her closet, revealing a light blue sapphire dress that shimmered in the sunlight. She adorned herself with a diamond necklace. She opened her cabin door and shouted out to Scabbage, telling him to put his evening attire on, and signaled to her first mate Patches to also change into his regal bodyguard attire.

They left the ship, taking side streets to make it appear as if they were coming from one of the plantations on the island. They made their way to the local tavern, plotting to seduce Captain Gabriel. All eyes were on Skye as she entered, her long golden locks cascading down her back and framing her heart-shaped face. The brilliant blue of her dress made her piercing blue eyes stand out even more, captivating all who looked upon her. She noticed some of her crew already stationed around the bar and took a seat at a nearby table. The barkeep hurried over to take her order and shooed away the bar wenches vying for attention. Skye ordered beef stew, a biscuit, and a glass of port wine. Her first mate stood guard at the door, surveying the room for any potential threats.

Finally, Captain Gabriel and his crew entered the tavern. He immediately locked eyes with Skye and was met with an intense stare back. Skye couldn't help but notice his striking features and was momentarily taken aback by his rugged charm. As he approached her table, she couldn't help but feel a flutter in her stomach. She introduced herself as Lady Sapphire of Nexten, passing through on her way to the Korkin Islands. Captain Gabriel smiled and revealed that he had traveled past those islands a few years ago. Skye smiled in agreement, and they struck up a conversation about their mutual love for sailing and adventure. He asked if he could join her for dinner, and she nodded eagerly. As they chatted, a flirty barmaid rushed over to take Captain Gabriel's order, much to Skye's annoyance. But she brushed it off, enjoying the company of this handsome captain from another world.

Captain Gabriel leaned back in his chair and asked Lady Sapphire, "Have you read any good literature lately?" They were both avid readers and had been enjoying a lively conversation about their favorite books and travels. Skye couldn't help but admire the Captain's intelligence and wit. Suddenly, the door burst open, and several of her crew members rushed in, causing a stir among Captain Gabriel's men. One of his officers approached him and whispered something in Danish before quickly leaving. Skye couldn't make out everything, but she heard them mention the name of the pirate they were searching for - herself.

She kept her cool as she sipped her drink, asking nonchalantly if everything was alright. The captain apologized for cutting their evening short, stating that duty called. He kissed her hand and bid her farewell, hoping their paths would cross again soon. Skye smiled to herself knowing that it would be sooner than the captain thought. As they left to search for her, she calmly made her way back to her hidden ship where she quickly changed into her usual pirate attire and donned her black mask that concealed half of her face. She armed herself with swords and knives, making sure to grab anything else she may need for a fight.

Returning to the tavern, she saw Captain Gabriel's men scouring the area for her. She chuckled to herself at their ignorance - little did they know that she was standing right in front of them moments ago. Stepping out of the shadows, she confidently declared, "I hear you're looking for me."

The captain wasted no time in announcing that he was arresting her on Queen Ava's orders from Freden Land. Skye drew her swords without hesitation, ready to defend herself against these unjust accusations. Her crew stood by, following her strict orders not to interfere with the fight. Captain Gabriel seemed surprised that she had come alone until she interrupted him with a fierce strike of her sword, signaling the beginning of their intense battle.

Captain Gabriel watched as the notorious pirate, Captain Skye, single-handedly took down his entire crew. She moved with grace and precision, her dual swords slicing through flesh and bone effortlessly. But just as she was about to defeat Gabriel himself, she was outnumbered and captured. She was surrounded and threw her swords down. She saw her crew in the distance and shook her head no. Skye was put in shackles and taken to Captain Gabriel's ship.

Gabriel couldn't help but feel a sense of satisfaction as he stood on his ship's deck, watching the infamous pirate being brought aboard in shackles. He had been warned by a crew member that Skye planned to kidnap him for ransom, but she had underestimated his strength and cunning.

As they set sail toward Gabriel's homeland, he couldn't help but think of how each capture reminded him of Princess Kalieanna's death. He had been unable to save her from another pirate years ago, and now he sought vengeance against those who shared the same profession.

Meanwhile, Skye's own crew followed at a safe distance, awaiting the signal from their captain. Their plan was to stay a safe distance back. They were waiting for their captain's signal. They knew their captain was resourceful and would find a way out of this predicament.

The plan was to get Captain Skye captured and board the ship for Blackbeard's stolen telescope - the same one he took from her father. Inside the telescope, there was supposed to be a map leading to the legendary Sapphire Stone. Skye knew that as a woman, she was underestimated by her male adversaries and could use that to her advantage.

With a small tool kit hidden in her pocket, Skye managed to pick the lock on her cell and make her way out of the brig. She headed towards the galley in search of something to signal her waiting crew. Grabbing a mop and some rags, she lit it on fire and stuck it out of a porthole. Hoping that her crew saw the smoke and understood her signal, Skye made her way to the deck. On the deck, she could hear the shouts of Danish men as they spotted her ship in the distance and began gaining on them. But thanks to Skye's modifications, including faster speeds and more accurate cannons, their ship was able to hold its own.

As they neared the enemy's ship flying a red flag, Skye remembered that her crew had voted to take no prisoners. But as cannonballs began flying and shaking their ship, she had more pressing matters at hand - getting to the captain's quarters.

Using her lock-picking skills once again, Skye managed to enter the cabin, where she found an impressive collection of books and artwork. But what she was searching for was not immediately visible. She picked another lock on the desk and finally found Blackbeard's telescope.

Just as she was about to secure it to herself, she heard a commotion outside and realized that Captain Gabriel's men had discovered her escape from the cell. Should she hide or fight? Skye quickly grabbed her swords and prepared for battle.

But before she could decide on a course of action, more cannon fire erupted outside, signaling that it was time for them to leave. Skye knew she had to act fast if she wanted to escape with the telescope and her life.

Skye strapped her two swords to her back, feeling the weight of their familiar metal against her skin. She needed to reach the deck and dive into the water to swim back to her ship. Before leaving the cabin, she peeked out to make sure the coast was clear. As she made her way down the hallway, Captain Gabriel appeared in front of her, blocking her path.

"You planned this whole thing, didn't you?" he accused, his eyes narrowing in anger. "To get captured and destroy my ship. All for what?"

"That's something you'll never know," Skye retorted confidently. With a swift move, she jumped up and grabbed onto a nearby pipe, using it to swing around and land a powerful kick on Gabriel's chest. He stumbled back but quickly regained his footing as Skye ran past him and dove into the sea.

She swam towards her ship, feeling a surge of pride at how quick and agile she was in the water. Her crew could see her approaching, and they cheered as she climbed aboard. With determination in her eyes, Skye commanded her men to open fire on Gabriel's ship with all their cannons.

As they watched the enemy ship slowly sink into the sea, Skye felt an odd twinge in her heart at the thought of never seeing Captain Gabriel again. It was strange since she barely even knew him.

But soon enough, a small boat arrived to pick Skye up from the water. Her first mate, Patches, greeted her with a huge smile, glad to see that their captain was safe and successful in her mission.

After confirming that the mission was indeed a success by showing him the stolen telescope, Skye's stern captain voice returned as she asked why they had flown the red flag during the attack.

Scabbage looked embarrassed and explained that Chef had convinced the crew to rally up and rescue their kidnapped captain by burning down Gabriel's ship. Skye was not impressed, as she had a plan in place and didn't need their interference. But it was too late now.

As they sailed back to their own ship, Skye shouted orders to Patches to change the flag, bring out more boats, and search for survivors from Gabriel's crew. The crew followed her commands, quickly rowing towards the sinking ship.

When everyone returned, Skye noticed that all of the crewmen from Gabriel's ship were accounted for except one. Scabbage explained that it was Ruit, the one who betrayed them. They weren't sure if he had survived or if he had hidden from them in fear of punishment.

Skye knew they would probably never find out what happened to him. But then Patches came running towards her, out of breath and urgent.

"Captain, Captain! Come quick!" he exclaimed. "What is it?" Skye asked, concerned.

"When we found Captain Gabriel, he was barely conscious and badly injured. Chef took him to the sick bay," Patches explained.

"What? You left him alone with Chef?" Skye shouted in frustration, knowing how skilled and dangerous Chef could be when angry.

But there was nothing she could do now except hope that Gabriel would survive and recover. And maybe have a stern talk with her crew about following orders in the future.

As Captain Skye entered the sick bay, she noticed Gabriel lying on the bed, unconscious. The wound on his leg was bleeding profusely. Without hesitation, she began to put pressure on the wound while calling for her assistant, Scabbaged, and Chef Javiour to fetch her supplies. With precision, she cleaned the wound with alcohol before carefully sewing it up with a needle and thread. She then applied healing herbs to the wound and monitored Gabriel's condition.

While sailing through Asia, Skye had learned various healing techniques and remedies, but she knew that Gabriel's recovery would take time. She thanked the Chef for his help and instructed him to start preparing food for the crew. After Skye patched up Gabriel, she knew there was nothing more to do but wait. She looked down at her outfit, and it was covered with Gabriel's blood. She told Scabbage that she was going to her cabin to change and he needed to watch over Captain Gabriel.

Leaving Scabbaged to watch over Gabriel, Skye went up on deck to give the crew their new heading - Paradise Island. It would take them two weeks to reach their destination, giving Skye enough time to work on deciphering the codes for her father's telescope. Skye made her way to her cabin. First thing she did was change her clothes she noticed there seemed to be a lot of blood. She hoped Gabriel was going to be okay.

After putting on clean, dry clothes, she went to her desk to work on the telescope. Skye carefully studied the telescope. It was gold and a foot long. When it was closed, when stretched out it was two feet. At the bottom of the telescope it has five different parts that need to be decoded. Remembering her father's advice to decipher one clue at a time, she focused on the first line of symbols. Her father had left her notes on how to decipher the codes. She reviewed her father's notes on the symbols on the first line. The first line said, "Red skies sailors delight." After some thought, she aligned the ship symbol with the calm waters symbol on the telescope and heard a click as the first compartment opened. She still had four more compartments to unlock.

The next clue proved to be more challenging - "Death and new beginnings." Skye thought of her own experiences with loss and starting anew before realizing that one of the symbols depicted a family - representing a new beginning for her and her father after they lost everything. Skye aligned the family symbol next to the Ship Symbol. She heard another click, and she was getting so excited. Soon, she would have her father's map of the Sapphire Stone. With a sense of determination, Skye continued working on unlocking each compartment in hopes of finding the elusive map that her father had left behind for her.

As Skye read her father's notes for the third clue, she couldn't help but feel overwhelmed. The symbols of family and death seemed to be connected somehow, but she was struggling to make sense of it. Suddenly, there was a knock on her cabin door. She yelled for the person to enter and in came her shipmate, Eric, with news that Captain Gabriel had regained consciousness. Skye rushed to Sick Bay, relieved to see that he was okay. But when he looked at her and asked who she was, she felt a pang of guilt. Gabriel seemed disorientated. He asked where he was and who all of us were.

Skye asked him, "Do you know your name?"

Gabriel thought for a minute and then replied, "No. I can't remember anything."

Skye said it must be from the gash on his head. Maybe when the swelling goes down, he will remember. Should I tell him that s had been the one to blow up his ship?

No, she decided to leave that part out for now. Instead, she explained that they had rescued him and his crew from their sinking ship. She explained that he was the captain of the ship, his name was Gabriel Wateman and he worked for the Queen's Navy.

Chef noticed a gash on Skye's arm and told her he was going to get the first aid kit. Skye said she was fine. Chef ignored her and tended to a gash on Skye's arm; she instructed Scabbage not to let Gabriel talk to any of his crew members to keep him isolated. Later, as she informed Gabriel's crew about his recovery and gave them a choice to join her crew or be let off at the next port like true pirates do, Skye couldn't help but feel grateful for Chef's fatherly concern towards her well-being. With everything going on, it was comforting to have someone looking out for her like that. Skye decided to go back to her cabin and think.

Skye's boots thudded against the wooden floor of her cabin as she paced back and forth, trying to figure out what to do about Gabriel. She knew he would be angry and possibly even try to harm her if he found out she had betrayed him. To keep an eye on him, she decided to have him dine with her in her cabin instead of allowing him to eat with the rest of the crew. As she sat at her desk, she absentmindedly picked up a small telescope and gazed through it as she thought.

Her mind drifted back to the third clue she had been working on before the interruption regarding Gabriel's condition. The symbols depicted sharks, decoys, and death, but Skye couldn't seem to make sense of them. She focused on the sharks first, remembering that they often traveled in groups known as a shiver or school. She moved the corresponding symbol into place on the map.

Next was the clue for the decoy, and Skye pondered over its meaning. It could refer to a lure or trap, both things that mermaids were known for using to entice sailors. But there was also a fishing net depicted, which could also be considered a trap. Frustrated, Skye pushed the thoughts aside as there was a knock on her door.

In walked Patches, one of her loyal crew members and first mate who always seemed to be in good spirits no matter how dire the situation. He announced that dinner orders were being taken for their upcoming supply stop. Skye's choices were limited - fried chicken, baked chicken, or boiled chicken. Patches joked about there always being some form of chicken on the menu and asked if Gabriel would be joining her for dinner.

Skye hesitated before finally deciding that having Gabriel join her would be beneficial. After all, he was quite intelligent and may hold valuable information regarding the mysterious telescope they had been searching for. She informed Patches that she would like to eat at 7, knowing how temperamental the ship's chef could be.

As Patches left, Skye returned to her task, deciding to skip over the decoy clue for now and move on to the one about death. She mused over all of the different interpretations of death - dying, killed, end, passing - and wondered which one was the key to unlocking the telescope's secrets.

Just as she was deep in thought, there was another knock on her door. Gabriel entered, announcing that he had been ordered to dine with the captain. Skye couldn't help but laugh at his formal language. She assured him it wasn't an order and he was free to leave if he wished. But Gabriel insisted it would be an honor to dine with her.

Before they could continue their conversation, Skye's stomach growled loudly, reminding her of the upcoming dinner. She told Gabriel that the food may not be up to his standards, but he replied that anything was better than being locked up in a cell. With a smile, Skye motioned for him to take a seat as they waited for dinner to be served.

In the dimly lit cabin, Skye placed a bottle of Italian wine and two glasses on the small dining table. Gabriel smiled and nodded in appreciation. As she turned to retrieve the glasses, he noticed the papers and symbols scattered across her desk. Curiosity getting the best of him, he asked about them. Skye explained that they were clues left by her late father, who had hidden a telescope for her to find and decipher. She was stuck on a clue involving a shark, a decoy, and death. Gabriel offered his puzzle-solving skills to help her out.

After examining the symbols, he suggested that "death" could also mean a new beginning. Skye's eyes widened as she realized the sunrise symbol could represent this new beginning. With renewed determination, she arranged the symbols and unlocked the telescope. Overjoyed, she hugged Gabriel before being interrupted by the arrival of dinner. As they ate the delicious meal prepared by their Chef, Gabriel noticed Skye's impressive collection of books and she shared with him her love for reading instilled by her father. As their hug ended, Skye's cheeks flushed with a mix of emotions.

Chef walked into the cabin, smiling as he pretended not to notice the intimate moment between his two guests. He set down dishes on the dining table - fresh rolls of chicken and pickled green beans. The aroma filled the room, and Skye couldn't help but exclaim how wonderful it smelled.

"I can't wait to dig in," she said with a smile.

Then she turned to Chef and asked playfully,

"Are you checking up on me? You usually send Patches or Scabbage with my meals."

Chef stuttered before admitting that he just needed a break from the kitchen. Skye chuckled and responded, "Well, I appreciate it. And it looks like you almost forgot about dessert!"

Chef's face lit up as he revealed a decadent chocolate cake. Skye thanked him for the sweet surprise before inviting Gabriel to take a seat at the table. He gallantly replied, "Ladies first." Skye graciously sat down and they both dug into the delicious meal in front of them. As they ate, Gabriel noticed the impressive collection of books lining the walls of the cabin.

"You must be quite the reader," he commented. Skye smiled proudly and explained that her father had insisted on her education - reading, writing, map-reading, and ancient history were all skills she possessed, thanks to his determination. Gabriel looked surprised by this revelation, and Skye couldn't resist teasing him, saying, "Did you think all pirates were illiterate?"

Gabriel's head bobbed in agreement, his long, tangled hair falling into his face. Skye noticed the faint smell of smoke and saw the worry lines etched on his forehead.

"You know, some say pirates are illiterate," he said.

Skye scoffed, "You can't believe everything you hear."

Gabriel rose from his seat and wandered towards the bookshelf. His eyes landed on a chess board set up on a small table nearby. "Do you play?" he asked.

Skye smiled, flicking her wrist over her shoulder to reveal a silver watch with intricate gears. "Quite well, actually. And yourself?"

Gabriel laughed, running his fingers through his unkempt hair. "I may not remember my name or where I'm from, but I do know how to play chess."

"Let's have a game then if you're not too tired," Skye suggested, gesturing towards the board.

"I am not tired; I think I will be fine," Gabriel said worriedly, still recovering from his injuries.

"You're fine," Skye reassured him with a gentle pat on the back.

They played for hours, each move calculated and strategic. Skye was impressed by Gabriel's skill and it kept her on her toes until she finally called checkmate.

Gabriel laid his queen down in defeat but wore a proud smile. "You are an exceptional player," he praised her.

Just as they were about to start another round, there was a knock at Skye's cabin door. She invited the person in, and Scabbage appeared to pick up their dinner plates before escorting Gabriel back to Sick Bay.

Before leaving, Gabriel took Skye's hand and kissed it lightly. "Thank you for a lovely night. I hope we can do this again sometime," he said sweetly.

Skye couldn't help but smile at his charm and replied, "Yes, we must do this again." "Perhaps I can also help you with that puzzle you were working on earlier," Gabriel added.

As they left, Skye couldn't help but think it was a perfect evening, except for the fact that when Gabriel regained his memories, he would surely want her dead.

After getting ready for bed, Skye lit a candle next to her bedside and continued reading her book. But she was awoken by a knock on her cabin door, which was unusual for her since she normally slept through the night. In a groggy state, she replied, "Enter."

In came Scabbage carrying her breakfast on a tray. He grinned at her and asked, "Did the princess oversleep?"

Skye rolled her eyes and retorted, "Very funny. What's for breakfast today?"

Scabbage explained that the chef had informed them they were running low on supplies and rationing the food now. They still had two days left before reaching their destination of Paradise Cove. Skye glanced down at her plate and saw the meager portions. It seemed like it was going to be another long day at sea.

Skye sat at the small table in her cabin, enjoying her usual breakfast of two fluffy biscuits, a dollop of jam, and a cup of steaming tea. Today, she skipped the usual cured meat and eggs.

"So no bacon or eggs today?" her first mate Scabbage asked, knowing her routine well.

"This will do," Skye replied with a contented sigh.

After finishing her breakfast, she headed out to check on her crew and the new members. As captain, it was her responsibility to ensure everyone's well-being. She made her way up to the upper deck and greeted each crew member with a smile. The sails were unfurled, catching the perfect breeze as they sailed towards Paradise Cove. Skye couldn't help but feel excited at the thought of returning home soon.

However, she also felt a twinge of sadness, knowing that Gabriel would be leaving the ship. It was for the best, though; he needed to leave before his memories returned, and he remembered that she had sunk his ship and nearly killed him. As she walked around the deck, checking on everything, Skye turned towards Sick Bay. She had been avoiding it, not wanting to face Gabriel after what happened between them. But as captain, she knew she had to check on him. When she walked in, panic set in as the room was empty.

What if Gabriel had somehow found out about their past? Then she heard laughter coming from the kitchen nearby and relaxed when she saw Chef and Gabriel covered in flour. She couldn't help but laugh at the sight. Gabriel was sitting on a stool while Chef bustled around the kitchen.

"What's going on here?" Skye asked with amusement.

"Gabriel is helping me in the kitchen," Chef replied proudly.

"He's showing me ways to preserve food and sharing some delicious recipes." Skye's heart swelled with happiness at seeing her crew working together and getting along.

It seemed that Gabriel was fitting in just fine. Gabriel's laughter echoed through the galley as he and Skye recounted the flour mishap that had earned them both a scolding from the chef. Despite the mess, they were relieved to have made it to their destination earlier than planned.

As they laughed, Skye invited Gabriel to join her for dinner that evening. He eagerly accepted, saying it would be most joyful, causing Skye to wonder what he meant by saying it would be "most joyful."

Meanwhile, Gabriel realized he needed to freshen up before their evening together. Returning to his quarters, Gabriel was greeted by Scabbage, who offered him a change of clothes after hearing about his kitchen fiasco. Grateful for the gesture, Gabriel chuckled at Scabbage's teasing reminder to have a "joyful" evening with Skye. In her own cabin, Skye carefully chose a light blue dress to wear for dinner, wanting to make an impression on Gabriel. She struggled with tying the back laces of her dress and was surprised when she opened the door to ask Scabbage for help, only to find Gabriel standing there instead.

Blushing, Skye stammered out her request for help and turned around so Gabriel could lace up her dress. As he worked on the delicate ribbons, he couldn't help but feel like he had done this before for a sister he didn't remember having. Skye complimented him on his skilled hands, causing him to playfully retort that he was probably better at taking things off rather than putting them on. After finishing with her dress, Gabriel couldn't take his eyes off of Skye, telling her she looked breathtaking. She returned the compliment and they headed off to dinner together, excitement building between them for what the evening might hold.

Skye ran her fingers through her wind-tousled hair and smoothed out the wrinkles in her crisp blue dress. Her eyes sparkled as she looked up at Gabriel, admiring his tailored jacket and deep blue tie that brought out the color of his piercing blue eyes. She returned his compliment with a smile, feeling a slight blush creep up her cheeks. Gabriel told her Scabbage loaned it to him. Skye replied that's where I had seen it before. He does like to dress up.

"Let's head inside before anyone starts wagging their tongues," Skye suggested, "Our dinner hasn't arrived yet, but would you like to help me work on this puzzle?"

Gabriel's grin widened, showing off his perfectly straight teeth. "I thought you'd never ask." Skye read him the next three clues: warning, beach, and night. She couldn't imagine how those symbols could fit together. But then Gabriel had an idea.

"What if we start with the warning? Like 'pink skies at night, sailor's delight'," he suggested, pointing to a clue with clouds and stars. Skye nodded in agreement.

"The beach must represent land," she added. "And the night could be the opposite - day."

They both exclaimed in excitement as they turned the telescope successfully and unlocked the fourth piece of the telescope. Skye was practically bouncing with joy, but she managed to contain herself when there was a knock on her cabin door.

It was Patches announcing that the Chef had prepared a stew with Gabriel's help and some delicious scones for dessert. They decided to pair it with a nice bottle of red wine. As soon as Patches left, Skye grabbed the telescope, Skye could barely contain herself; she grabbed Gabriel and kissed him. Gabriel was taken aback but quickly returned the kiss. Skye felt as if fireworks were going off in her head; as she was kissing Gabriel, they finally pulled away. Gabriel smiled and said if that had happened before, I would remember that. Skye's cheeks were flushed; she quickly gained her composure and suggested that they eat their dinner. Gabriel nodded.

As they sat down at the dining room table, Skye and Gabriel shared stories of their adventures at sea and the different places they had visited. To Skye's surprise, Gabriel asked her where she had learned to speak Danish.

"How did you know that?" she asked curiously.

"I heard you talking to your crew," he replied with a smile.

Skye chuckled. "My father made sure I learned many languages growing up since we traveled so much."

Laughter filled the ship's cabin as Gabriel and Skye played a game of chess. Their hands brushed against each other as they moved pieces on the board, sending chills down their spines. Gabriel couldn't resist taking Skye's hand in his and gazing into her mesmerizing sapphire eyes. The attraction between them was undeniable.

As they continued to chat and play, Gabriel couldn't shake the feeling that he knew Skye from somewhere before. But with his memory missing, he couldn't place where they might have met. He made a mental note to explore the ship tomorrow and see if any of the crew recognized him.

But for now, he was content being in Skye's company. She was kind and understanding about his memory loss, offering words of reassurance that they would come back in time. But as they shared a passionate kiss, there was no denying the intense chemistry between them.

Their moment was interrupted by a knock on the cabin door, bringing them back to reality. Patches, one of the crew members, stood awkwardly at the door as Gabriel and Skye tried to compose themselves. Skye quickly found an excuse for Patches' presence and they said their goodnights.

As Gabriel left the cabin, trying to hide his arousal with a napkin, Skye couldn't help but admire his bulging pants. She knew she wanted him more than ever.

But as they both retired to their separate cabins for the night, Skye couldn't shake off the thought that once Gabriel regained his memories, everything could change between them.

Skye sat at her desk, sipping a glass of red wine and staring at the telescope. It was going to be a long night on the pirate ship. If Skye could get the last clue she could open the telescope and get the Sapphire Stone map and make her father so proud of her. She was going to need some help. She finally finished her drink and made her way to bed, hoping that her lover, Gabriel, would show up at some point. As she climbed into bed, there was a knock on her door. Skye's heart fluttered with excitement, thinking it was Gabriel. Instead, it was Scabbage, one of her fellow pirates. He could see the disappointment on his captain's face. He chuckled at her, sorry to disappoint, but he was here to pick up the stack of dirty dishes from dinner.

"You forgot those," she said.

She rolled her eyes and told him to go back and fetch them. But Scabbage warned her about getting too involved with Gabriel, reminding her that he would eventually remember that she had blown up his ship and stolen from him.

Skye shrugged off his warning, thanking him for his concern before shutting the door. But as she lay in bed, she couldn't stop thinking about Gabriel and their undeniable chemistry. She had been with many lovers before, but none had made her feel the way he did.

Just as she started to drift off to sleep, there was another knock on her door. This time, it was

Scabbage's, who always seemed to have a cheerful disposition.

"Rise and shine!" he exclaimed. "It's less than a day until I see Marguerite Again!" Marguerite was Scabbages' wife whom they hadn't seen in six months since being out at sea.

As they enjoyed breakfast together, Scabbage reminded Skye that there was more to life than just treasure and adventure. He talked about going home and being with his family.

But Skye scoffed at the idea, stating that her fellow pirates were her family and the ship Vixen was her home. However she did admit to enjoying spending time at her land home when they weren't pirating.

As the day went on, Skye couldn't get Gabriel out of her mind. She wondered what it would be like to make love to him and felt drawn to him despite Scabbage's warning. She knew she should keep her distance, but she couldn't resist the temptation. That night, as they sailed towards their next adventure, Skye found herself lost in thoughts of Gabriel and what could have been if they weren't pirates constantly on the move.

Skye paced back and forth in her large cabin, her fists clenched at her sides. She couldn't shake the image of Gabriel's soft lips pressed against hers. But he was a man of honor, unlike her and the rest of her pirate crew. She had to push him away, even if it hurt. Suddenly, there was a knock on her door and she quickly shouted for them to wait while she got dressed. Patches, her first mate, stood outside with a sly smirk on his face.

"Good morning, captain," he said. "Our prisoner, aka your boyfriend Gabriel, is requesting an audience with you."

Skye glared at him, annoyed by his teasing tone. "He is not my boyfriend," she snapped. Patches chuckled. "If you say so. What shall I tell him?"

"Tell him to come at noon," Skye replied. "I have to check on the crew and make sure we're not being followed. We just sunk a queen's naval ship."

Once Patches left, Skye sighed and turned her attention back to the desk where her father's treasure map lay. She knew she was getting closer to finding it, but she needed to focus on her duties as captain first.

Making her way up to the deck, Skye took over the helm and let the wind blow through her hair. She missed the feeling of steering the ship and the sense of freedom it brought. As they sailed closer to land, Skye could see seagulls flying overhead and smell the saltwater in the air. She felt alive and free for a moment, forgetting all about Gabriel and their complicated situation.

Meanwhile, in sickbay, Gabriel couldn't get Skye out of his mind. He had been with many women before, but none had affected him like she did. He leaned back against the wall, lost in thought as he waited for his injuries to heal.

As his memories continued to elude him, Gabriel couldn't shake the feeling that he was missing something important. That's why he couldn't wait to see Skye again, hoping she could help him piece together his past. But as he waited for her return to her cabin, he couldn't shake the nerves and uncertainty that plagued him.

Meanwhile, Skye returned to her cabin after spending the morning on deck. She freshened up, admiring the tan on her face that made her blue eyes shine even brighter. As she sat at her desk, there was a knock on the door, and Gabriel entered, unaccompanied by any of her crew members. He informed her that Patches had said some things he couldn't unsee, and that's why the crew had deemed him capable of finding his way to her cabin alone.

Skye invited him to sit down, and they chatted about their upcoming lunch while she showed him the progress she had made in solving the puzzle. They discussed the clues: home, directions, and bonds that tie. Skye explained how she had started working on them before needing to attend to her captain duties. Together, they looked at each symbol - a ship and a house for home, a ship wheel and compass for direction. After much deliberation, they decided that the compass must be the correct answer.

The last clue, bonds that tie, stumped both of them. Skye suggested a rope as a possible solution, but Gabriel pointed out that it could refer to several different things. They were still deep in discussion when their lunch arrived, giving them a chance to take a break from the intense puzzle-solving.

Skye carefully lined up the symbols one by one. The picture of her childhood home, the compass that always guided her, and the bonds of family that held her together. As she turned the telescope, a map suddenly flew out onto the floor. Excitedly, she grabbed Gabriel and kissed him deeply while he willingly reciprocated. Their clothes came off in a flurry as they gave in to their passion. The heat of their bodies was intense, and when they finally came together, it was like an explosion of pleasure. They lay there in silence, trying to catch their breath, both afraid to speak for fear of breaking the magic of the moment.

After a few minutes, Skye's thoughts were interrupted by Gabriel's voice whispering, "I want you."As they entwined, their bodies radiated heat, and Skye was overwhelmed by the intensity of the moment. She couldn't recall ever experiencing such a powerful climax. Gabriel struggled to control himself but finally succumbed to the pleasure, his body shaking with ecstasy as he released it. They both lay there in silence, trying to catch their breaths. Skye's throat felt parched, and she rose to her feet, planning to get some water. But Gabriel stopped her, saying they weren't finished yet. As she smiled and reached for some watered-down rum, he noticed a birthmark on her upper thigh that seemed familiar.

Had they been together before? Despite the familiar sensation between them, it still felt like their first time. Just then, there was a knock at the door. Skye quickly grabbed a white silk robe to cover herself before answering. It was Patches, grinning at her strange choice of attire for the middle of the day. Skye blushed and made up an excuse about spilling wine on her outfit.

Patches laughed and left, saying they would be at the shore in a few hours. As Skye brought a tray of food over to the table, she asked Gabriel if he was hungry. He replied that he was famished but not for food; he wanted more of her instead. "I think you should save your energy," she teased him with a mischievous smile. Skye's body buzzed with anticipation as she leaned in to kiss Gabriel. The second time they made love, their hands roamed slowly, tracing every curve and dip of one another's skin. They moaned in unison as their bodies found a rhythm, building towards an explosive climax that left them both breathless and spent. As they lay tangled in the sheets, Skye couldn't help but think how perfect this moment was.

But their blissful moment was soon interrupted by a knock on the door. "I need five minutes," Skye called out before hurrying to get dressed. She brushed her hair quickly and told Gabriel to stand by the desk while she answered the door.

It was Scabbage, the ship's steward, here to pick up their lunch dishes. Skye explained that they had gotten lost in solving the puzzle on the telescope and completely forgot to eat. Scabbage chuckled when he saw the messy bed and said jokingly, "Looks like you were working on something else." Skye blushed but let him leave the food tray for her ravenous appetite.

As they ate, Skye spread out the map of the Sapphire Stone on the desk. Her heart raced at the thought that they were actually looking at a real treasure map. According to them, they needed to get to Mystic Island.

She grabbed a book from her bookshelf titled "The Mysteries of the Sapphire Stone" and opened it up to reveal a more detailed map of Mystic Eye Island. Skye studied it carefully, trying to determine the best route for their journey.

Suddenly, she heard her crew yelling that they were approaching the dock. She knew they didn't have much time left together before Gabriel would have to leave. But she also knew that finding the Sapphire Stone was worth everything. With determination in her heart, she grabbed an atlas map from near Mystic Eye Island and prepared for their next adventure.

The ship sailed smoothly through the narrow opening of the caves, its skilled captain Skye at the helm. The crew worked together to secure the ship to the dock and release vines to cover the entrance, hiding them from any passersby. As they cheered and celebrated their safe arrival, Skye addressed her crew, giving them orders for their fortnight stay in Paradise Cove. She reminded them of the dangers that awaited them as they set off in search of the coveted Sapphire Stone.

As her crew went off to enjoy some much-needed rest and relaxation, Skye turned her attention to Gabriel and his crew. She instructed him to go into town where they could find accommodations and provisions thanks to the trade business on the island. Skye even handed him some gold coins to cover their expenses.

As Gabriel expressed his gratitude, Skye couldn't help but wonder why none of his crew had told him about her role in sinking his previous ship. She glanced at his crew, who seemed just as surprised by this revelation. With a polite farewell, Skye walked away, grateful for Gabriel's help with the telescope despite their complicated past.

Gabriel's heart ached as he stood on the edge of the island, watching Skye walk away. He called out her name, and she turned around with a hopeful look in her eyes. "What if I don't want to go home?" he shouted, his heart racing. "I want to come with you and find the treasure."

Skye's heart skipped a beat at his words. She wanted nothing more than for him to join her, but she feared that once his memories returned, he would hate her for taking him away from his life. But before she could respond, Gabriel grinned. Skye said, "Well, what kind of host would I be if I didn't invite you to my plantation for a nice home-cooked meal?"

With a smile on her face, Skye led him through fields of vibrant flowers - purple, blue, bright red, and sparkling pink - until they reached a beautiful house perched on top of a hill. Corinthian columns adorned the front entrance, and a sprawling deck offered breathtaking views. Gabriel couldn't believe how magnificent it all was.

As they approached the house, they were greeted by a group of children ranging from ages 5 to 12, who ran up to Skye with hugs and requests for presents. Skye laughed I forgot to get you any gifts. When they all sighed disappointedly, she playfully scolded them by asking if they had been good while she was gone. They all nodded eagerly.

"Well then," Skye said with a mischievous twinkle in her eye, "let me see what I might have in my bag." She pulled out bags of chocolate, and the children squealed with joy as she passed them out.

As the children gleefully ran off with their treats, Gabriel noticed that Skye's face softened, and her guard came down. She was a different person than he had seen before. Their estate overseer, Cavay, approached them and gave Skye a warm hug. As he called her Lady Sapphire, Gabriel felt a sense of familiarity but couldn't place it. Skye introduced him as Captain Gabriel Wateman, rescued by her crew after his ship sank and suffering from amnesia. Cavay was taken aback but maintained his composure and welcomed Gabriel to the island.

Their head housekeeper, Baya, greeted them and took their luggage upstairs to the guest room. Cavay asked if they needed to prepare a separate room for the captain or if he would be sharing Skye's bedroom. Skye nonchalantly replied that it was up to the captain. With a smile, Gabriel expressed his desire to share quarters with the lady.

Cavay then informed Skye that dinner would be served soon and asked if she needed time to freshen up and change. Skye nodded and excused herself to her luxurious bedroom. As they entered, Gabriel couldn't help but admire the intricately carved mahogany bed, matching furniture, and a walk-in closet filled with beautiful dresses of all colors and styles.

After choosing a simple floral dress, Skye offered to show Gabriel the shower which was larger than most bathrooms he had seen. The gold fixtures caught his eye as Skye joked about being a successful pirate. They playfully lathered each other up in the spacious shower before getting ready for dinner together.

Skye stood in front of Gabriel with a sly smile, slowly undressing as she spoke. "I'm going to take a shower. Care to join me?" she asked, her eyes sparkling with mischief. Without waiting for an answer, she walked towards the large bathroom and turned on the water, beckoning for Gabriel to follow. The shower was opulent, with gold fixtures and plenty of space for two people. Skye playfully teased Gabriel about her pirate profession paying well and offered to lather him up. As they washed each other, their playful banter turned more intimate, and they couldn't resist giving in to their desires. After drying off and getting dressed, Skye handed Gabriel a blue lava and shirt to wear for the day. He was unfamiliar with how to wear it, but Skye expertly tied it around his waist in the traditional manner. She joked about being better at taking them off than putting them on and suggested asking Cavay for help if needed.

When Gabriel asked about undergarments, Skye laughed and explained that it was customary to not wear any. Skye herself wore a flattering floral print dress without a bra or underwear underneath. As they left the bedroom, Gabriel felt slightly uncomfortable with the idea of going commando but also enjoyed the feeling of freedom and possibility with Skye. Gabriel felt a surge of excitement and arousal as Skye led him into the grand dining room, her hand resting lightly on his arm. The table was a magnificent mahogany, with intricate carvings and enough seating for an entire village. Skye explained that her father, the captain of the Vixen was known here as the Duke, loved to host lavish parties for the townspeople and had quite the reputation for his generosity and protection over them. But since his passing two years ago, Skye hadn't felt up to throwing any parties. That is, until now. With the map finally retrieved and their quest almost complete, Skye couldn't help but feel a glimmer of festive spirit. Maybe they could plan a party together and invite the whole town to celebrate their success.

As they sat down at the head of the table, Gabriel couldn't help but notice Skye's elegance and grace as she settled into her seat. Baya, the chef and a close friend of Skye's father served them a steaming bowl of squash soup. Skye complimented the delicious aroma and thanked Baya for the meal. When Gabriel asked if this was the same chef from the ship, Skye nodded and explained that he was like family to her and had promised her father on his deathbed to always watch out for her.

Next came deviled cheese balls, one of Skye's favorite dishes. As she savored each bite, Gabriel couldn't help but admire how beautiful she looked when she smiled. They chatted about their love for literature and discovered that they shared a passion for adventure novels.

Skye couldn't believe how easily she was opening up to Gabriel, considering they had only known each other for a short time. But then again, she had saved his life, and they had been intimately together.

As they finished their meal, Skye couldn't help but hope that this wasn't just a fleeting moment. She knew Gabriel would soon regain his memories and return to his life as an officer of the law while she would continue her life as a pirate. But for now, she couldn't help but enjoy their time together and hope for the best.

Skye leaned in, the flickering candlelight casting shadows across her face. "My father had a love for artwork," she said as Gabriel listened intently. "He would steal it whenever he had the chance - paintings, vases, statues. He had a keen eye for it all."

Gabriel chuckled. "Your father truly had great taste. I feel like I'm in a royal castle."

Skye smiled and took a sip of her wine. "He did treat me like a princess, but he also taught me how to fight with swords and knives and use my opponent's weight against them." As they waited for the next course, Baya brought out a platter of fried chicken, mashed potatoes with gravy, and homemade biscuits. The smell made their stomachs growl, and they dug in eagerly.

"This is delicious," Skye said between bites.

Baya cleared their plates and offered them tea with lemon tart for dessert. Skye was so full, but she couldn't resist the sweet treat. "Baya, could you please bring it to the parlor? We'll adjourn there after dinner."

They made their way to the cozy parlor, complete with an unlit fireplace and a chessboard set up on a table. Skye poured them each a glass of brandy from the impressive selection on display.

"I think part of the legend on the treasure map is written in Sumerian," Skye said, pulling out the wrinkled paper from her pocket. "We'll need an interpreter when we get there."

Gabriel nodded in agreement as Skye called for Cavay to send for the island's resident history buff and language expert known as the Professor. Gabriel and Skye enjoyed their brandy and talked about the different artwork in the room. Skye told him various stories about how her father had maintained some of them; Baya came into the parlor and announced that the professor was there.

Soon enough, Professor Wolfram entered the parlor looking disheveled with his nose buried in a book. "I have a proposition for you," Skye said as he sat down.

The professor's eyes lit up at the mention of a challenge. "Tell me more." Skye's heart raced as she approached the professor at the library, clutching the ancient book in her hands. She could feel her father's presence with every turn of the page. The professor's eyebrows furrowed in confusion as he recognized the book.

"Why are you showing me this? Your father showed it to me all the time," he said with a hint of annoyance. Ignoring his skepticism, Skye pulled out a map from her bag and spread it out on the table. As the professor examined it, his eyes widened with excitement.

"The legends are true! There is a map!" he exclaimed in awe.

Skye nodded, a sly smile forming on her lips. "That's why I called for you," she replied. It was then that she introduced him to Captain Gabriel Wateman of the Queen's Navy, who was staying with her while recovering from his injuries and memory loss. The three of them quickly formed a plan to embark on a treasure hunt together, with the professor providing crucial knowledge and expertise. As they discussed preparations for their journey, Skye couldn't help but feel drawn to Gabriel, his strong arms and piercing blue eyes captivating her every move.

As night fell, they retired to Skye's bedroom, unable to keep their hands off each other as they undressed in a frenzy. The passion between them was intense and unyielding as they made love right inside the door, too consumed by a desire to make it to the bed. As they lay entwined in each other's arms, Skye woke to soft kisses on her neck and a hand exploring her body. She eagerly reciprocated, eager for more of Gabriel's touch. It felt like they were under some kind of spell, unable to resist each other's charms for even a moment. Just when things were getting heated, there was a quiet knock on the door.

"Do you want breakfast, my lady?" a voice called from outside.

Skye chuckled and pulled the covers up to cover their naked bodies. "Yes, thank you, Cavay," she replied with a sly grin before returning her attention to Gabriel. Cavay stepped inside. He asked if she would like breakfast on the terrace outside her room or on the breakfast table in her room. Skye eagerly chose the terrace, wanting to take advantage of the beautiful morning. As she got dressed, Gabriel emerged from his room wearing a soft silk robe in a deep royal blue. Skye followed suit with her own magenta silk robe, and they headed out to the terrace together.

Cavay brought out a tray of fruit and crumpets, along with some tea, for their breakfast. They enjoyed each other's company as they ate and then decided to spend some time at the beach, taking advantage of the warm sunshine and indulging in some passionate moments in the waves.

Over the next few days, Skye and Gabriel grew closer and enjoyed getting to know each other better. But their peaceful time was interrupted when Baya burst into their room one afternoon. Both Skye and Gabriel were taken aback by his sudden presence.

Baya caught his breath and explained that while checking on supplies at the dock, he saw a Queen's Navy ship pull into port. The admiral was asking about none other than Captain Gabriel and the infamous pirate captain known as Skye.

Skye felt a wave of panic wash over her. How had they discovered her island? There must be a traitor among her crew. She pushed those thoughts away for now and focused on changing into more appropriate attire for her guest's arrival.

Meanwhile, Gabriel couldn't believe it. It seemed like he might finally get some answers about his past and possibly even discover who he truly was. Skye excused herself to change, suggesting that Gabriel do the same.

A sharp knock echoed through the grand foyer of the mansion, and Skye quickly straightened her dress and smoothed down her hair. She took a deep breath and walked towards the front door, where she could hear Cavay greeting their guests - Admiral William Hitchcock and six of his officers. Skye greeted them warmly and invited them to take a seat in the lavish parlor. As they settled into the plush chairs, the admiral began to explain the reason for their visit - they were investigating the disappearance of naval officer Gabriel Watemen, whose ship had been mysteriously blown up. The admiral revealed that they believed it was the notorious pirate Captain Skye who had attacked Gabriel's ship and killed the entire crew. Skye gasped in shock and disbelief at the accusation, denouncing such savage behavior from pirates. The admiral reassured her that they didn't believe she would come here, but just as he finished speaking, a familiar voice called out from behind them. It was Gabriel himself, walking into the parlor with a slight limp but otherwise unscathed. The admiral and his officers were stunned to see him alive and well.

As they exchanged greetings, Gabriel looked around in confusion, not recognizing anyone in the room except for Skye. She quickly jumped to explain that they had rescued Gabriel and his crew after finding them stranded at sea. She mentioned that Gabriel had suffered a head injury resulting in memory loss. The admiral then stepped forward to introduce himself as an old friend who had married Gabriel's sister, Katie. He reminded Gabriel of their shared childhood memories and how he was now an uncle to their two children, Henric and Eric. But Gabriel couldn't recall any of it, causing worry among his fellow officers. One of them, Officer William Blackman, approached him and tried to jog his memory by reminding him of all the mischief they got into during grade school. But even this didn't seem to ring a bell for Gabriel. With a confused look on his face, he asked the admiral about the information they had gathered - that Captain Skye, the notorious pirate, had blown up his ship to obtain a treasure map hidden aboard. The admiral confirmed that their source was reliable. Skye's expression quickly changed from shock to confusion, mirroring Gabriel's thoughts. She then invited the group to stay for dinner, hoping to diffuse the tense situation. The admiral accepted gratefully; Skye suggested going to the parlor for some before-dinner drinks. The admiral nodded; that would be lovely, and if it was not too formal to pay you a compliment, Lady Sapphire, you look radiant.

She chose a vibrant yellow dress with delicate lace from Italy, trying to look the part of a governess rather than a notorious pirate captain. Skye made her way to the parlor to await her unwelcome guest, already instructing Cavay to notify the crew that they would be leaving earlier than planned and to start preparing.

The admiral smiled warmly, thanking Skye for her hospitality as she showed him to the game/parlor room. "I'll have one of my staff take your drink orders," she told him with a polite smile. "We have an excellent selection of wines, ports, whiskey - whatever you prefer." She excused herself to inform the chef of the dinner party, but Gabriel followed her out and wouldn't let her escape until he got some answers.

"Lady Sapphire," he called after her in a firm tone. "May I have a word with you before you attend to your staff?" Skye's smile tightened, but she nodded. They stepped away from the kitchen so their conversation would not be overheard by the admiral and his men.

Gabriel's eyes bore into hers as he asked the question that had been burning in his mind. "Did you blow up my ship and steal the treasure map?" Skye was taken aback, shocked that he would even think such a thing. She fumbled for an answer, but Gabriel could see the truth in her eyes.

"It was before I knew you before we became involved," she tried to explain. "Today, I would have just asked for it." Anger flashed across Gabriel's features as he yelled at her.

"All you care about is your precious treasure! You don't care who gets hurt in the process. I could have been killed; my men could have been killed!" He stormed off towards the door, threatening to go straight to the admiral and reveal Skye's true identity.

Skye begged him not to, explaining that if she were arrested, the island and its people would be left vulnerable. To her relief, Gabriel relented, knowing that innocent lives could be at stake if he revealed her secret.

As soon as he left, Skye knew what she needed to do. She gathered her crew and informed them that it was time to leave. The ship was already stocked with supplies and weapons - she had just been stalling for more time with Gabriel.

She quickly changed into her pirate attire with a mask in case any of the navy crew were about. She wanted to make sure it was easy to move in before slipping out to meet her crew. Skye made her way down to the docks through the brush; she went to the cave where her ship, Vixen, was hidden. She saw most of the crew was already there waiting and to avoid the Naval guard. She told them of their plans to set sail after sundown, and Skye made sure to inform the professor so he could be ready as well. Patches asked about the admiral and his crew. Skye told him not to worry about it; she had a surprise in store for them. As she prepared to leave back to the house, she couldn't help but feel a pang of regret for deceiving Gabriel and leaving him behind. But duty called, and she knew what she had to do. She made her way back to the house.

Skye quietly slipped into her bedroom, carefully closing the door behind her. She quickly changed into a light powder blue dress that she could easily slip in and out of without help. As she finished getting dressed, she wondered where Gabriel was. She knew he had been angry with her earlier, but she was relieved that he hadn't told the admiral about their secret relationship.

Just as Skye opened her door, she found Gabriel standing outside in a handsome navy blue suit that his friend Cavay had picked out for him. He suggested they go to dinner together so it wouldn't look suspicious. Skye agreed, and they made their way to the game room, where they could hear laughter coming from inside.

As they entered the room, all eyes turned to Skye. She looked breathtaking in her dress. She greeted the men and invited them to join them in the dining room, where the table had been set with fine china and silverware by Cavay.

The first course was a refreshing fruit and green salad with a delicious vinaigrette dressing. The main meal was beef stew with potatoes and carrots, accompanied by homemade biscuits. The men couldn't stop raving about how delicious the food tasted. But while everyone else seemed to be enjoying their meal, Skye noticed that Gabriel barely touched his food and seemed lost in thought. In reality, he was thinking about his walk and how betrayed he felt when he learned that Skye had been lying to him all this time. Was it all part of some ploy to make him forgive her? He couldn't shake off his feelings of hurt and betrayal, even as he tried to put on a brave face for everyone else at the table.

As dinner came to an end, Gabriel's memories started coming back in bits and pieces. He knew he needed to tell Skye about what he remembered so far — including his mother's name — but he wasn't sure if he was ready to face the truth just yet.

As they finished their dinner, Gabriel could feel the weight of his secrets and betrayal pressing down on him. Skye's carefree laughter only added to his guilt as he watched her entertain their guests. He knew that with the destruction of his ship, the bounty on her head had increased twofold. Part of him still wanted to turn her in and collect the reward, but when he looked at her, all thoughts of betrayal vanished from his mind. The servants cleared away their plates, revealing warm, fruit-filled cobblers for dessert. But as each man took a bite, they slumped over lifelessly, revealing that Skye had drugged them all with the help of the chef. Gabriel stood up in shock and anger, accusing her of caring only about treasure and not human life. Gabriel shouted now you are murdering innocent men. Skye calmly explained that they were not dead, they were given a sleeping potion. They would wake up in a few hours. Gabriel asked why he was not given the sleeping potion. Skye calmly revealed that she had no intention of harming him because she trusted him not to betray her. She gave him a choice - stay with his sleeping crew or join her on a treasure hunt. Gabriel knew deep down that he would go with her despite his initial plans to turn her in afterward. They made their way to the hidden location of their ship and found their crew ready to set sail. Patches were helping the professor gather supplies while Skye and Gabriel climbed aboard. With the atlas map, treasure map, and the professor's linguistic skills, they were all set for their adventure. Skye carefully drove her ship, Vixen, out of her hiding place to make it to open waters.

Skye stood confidently at the helm, her sharp eyes scanning the horizon as she barked out orders to her crew. The ship surged forward, leaving the admiral's vessel in its wake. Skye called for her first officer, Patches, to take over while she retreated to her cabin to study the map. As she entered, she was surprised to find Gabriel and a professor huddled over it. "Excuse me," Skye said with a laugh. "I believe this is my cabin," Gabriel smirked and explained that he was considering their options for reaching Mystic Island. One way led past treacherous mermaids who lured men to their deaths, another passed by King Neptune, who had a reputation for destroying ships, and the third option was through the tight and dangerous Erie Canal. Skye studied the map carefully before making her decision. Skye said we would sail at the bottom of Pirate's Cove through the Erie Canal. "We'll stay close to pirates," she declared, knowing that most of them were too occupied with women and drinks to pose a threat. "And besides, they know me well enough not to mess with me." But Gabriel pointed out that the recent bounty on Skye's head had doubled, making some pirates more willing to take the risk. Skye drew her sword and thrust it into the map near their chosen route. She was ready for whatever dangers lay ahead.

Skye sat at her desk, pouring over the ancient map and symbols. She was determined to decipher its secrets and find the hidden treasure that would make her rich beyond her wildest dreams. In the corner of her cabin, Patches set a plate of steaming food on a small table. "Will Captain Gabriel be joining you?" he asked with a knowing smirk. Skye's heart skipped a beat at the mention of his name, but she quickly composed herself and replied, "No, he's eating with the crew." As she pushed her food around on her plate, lost in thoughts of the handsome captain who had captured her heart. Suddenly, there was a knock at her door. Skye drew her sword and cautiously opened it, only to find Gabriel standing there with a slice of chocolate cake in hand. She couldn't believe it - he had brought dessert for her. As they embraced, Skye could feel his anger and hurt radiating from him. She knew she had lied to him about her true identity as a notorious pirate, but seeing him now made her regret everything. Could she ever make things right and convince him to forgive her? Or would their love be doomed by their different paths in life?

As they sat in the captain's quarters, Gabriel noticed the book that Skye had been reading. Curiosity getting the best of him, he asked if she had found any more clues. She replied with excitement, telling him about the mystical sapphire stone that grants one's heart's desire. Gabriel warned her to be careful, reminding her that greed could be her downfall and there is more to life than material possessions.

Skye snapped at him, stating that she would rather have all the wealth and power that come with the sapphire stone. But as they continued reading the book together, Gabriel pointed out a crucial detail: in order to achieve their desires, they must be willing to sacrifice their greatest treasure.

Skye confidently stated that it would be easy for her to give up her chase for the Sapphire Stone, but she had promised her dying father on his deathbed. Skye, a pirate, always keeps their word. So I will find the Sapphire Stone no matter the cost.

As they discussed their plan, Skye noticed their ship changing direction. They went up on deck and saw Scabbage at the helm, explaining that they were at the Erie Canal entrance to avoid being caught by the Naval guard. Skye took over navigation and enlisted someone to watch for rocks at the front of the boat. Gabriel volunteered to watch out for rocks. He quickly made his way from the port side of the ship to the bow in front of the ship. Skye stood at the helm of the ship, waiting for Gabriel to tell her the direction they needed to go. Gabriel shouted go towards the starboard side. Skye gently turns the ship to the right. Then Gabriel shouts port side. Skye quickly turns the ship to the left. This continues for a couple of hours. As night fell and visibility decreased, Skye ordered lanterns to be placed at the front of the ship. They navigated carefully through the canal, making sure not to damage their ship. To their relief, they saw that the naval ship stopped following them.

But Skye knew they couldn't let their guard down yet.

Meanwhile, Gabriel stood on the bow of the ship with a lantern in one hand and a telescope in the other, scanning for potential obstacles ahead. As they approached a particularly narrow and dangerous section of the canal, Skye couldn't help but hold her breath as she expertly steered their ship through, with Gabriel signaling for any necessary course corrections.

Finally, they made it through the Erie Canal unscathed. In a moment of relief and gratitude, Skye hugged Gabriel and thanked him for his invaluable navigation skills. He hugged her back with a smile, feeling grateful to have found a partner like Skye on this perilous journey.

Skye's heart raced as she remembered her deception and the consequences it brought. She stepped back from Gabriel, fear etched on his face as he excused himself and hurried out of the room. Breathing deeply, Skye turned to Scabbage and asked him to take over while she retreated to her cabin. Before heading to her cabin, she asked a couple of crew members to row a short climb to the top of the island to see if they could see the admiral's ship. Lefty and Lewis hurried on their way to do as the captain asked. She needed to know the admiral's exact location so she could come up with a plan to get by them. Skye made her way to her cabin and started thinking. She needed to focus on plotting their next move past King Neptune's territory.

Sitting at her desk, Skye poured over maps of Mystic Island and Pirates Cove, trying to find the safest route that wouldn't lead them straight into the Queen's Navy. The thought of encountering Admiral Hitchcock again filled her with dread. She knew he would be furious about her deception and the sleeping powder she had slipped into his stew. Of course, also blew up one of the queen's naval ships. Skye would have to be careful. The bounty on her head most likely has tripled, where maybe even one of her own crew members might be tempted to turn her in. Skye shuddered at the thought her crew was loyal to her but everyone had a price.

Determined to come up with a plan, Skye enlisted the help of Patches and Scabbage. There was a knock on the door. Skye said, "Enter." It was Lefty; he said Skye was right to believe that the Admiral's ship was waiting for them on the other side of the island. Lefty pointed to the map at the exact location of the ship. As they discussed their options, Gabriel and the professor walked in, accidentally leaving the door open. Skye quickly filled them in on her plans to get past the Queen's Navy undetected.

But they needed a distraction. Skye thought for a moment before coming up with an idea - they could dock where they were and row to shore with smoke bombs and weapons, creating a diversion to make it past Hitchcock's ship. They would need smoke bombs to create cover for their escape.

Heading up on deck, Skye rallied her crew, shouting for volunteers to stay behind and launch the explosive devices at Hitchcock's ship. With six brave men willing to stay behind and carry out the plan, Skye felt a glimmer of hope that they might make it safely to Mystic Island and claim the treasure.

But first, they needed ingredients for their smoke bombs. Skye consulted with the foul-tempered chef, who reluctantly shared his knowledge of making explosives. They would need parchment paper, sugar, and potassium nitrate - all items typically found in gunpowder.

After cooking the ingredients in a cast iron skillet and placing them in parchment paper with a wick, they were ready to launch their distraction. Skye and Patches gathered up the bombs and brought them up on deck. Skye could see the launcher was already in the row boat. She asked if any of you have matches. Lefty raised his hand and showed her the matches. Skye said okay, when you get up to the top of the hill, wait for my signal so we will be ready to leave as fast as we can. Also, the wicks are long, but be careful, and timing is everything. We want the admiral's ship completely covered with smoke and for him to believe he is being attacked. So after you fired all the bombs, you need to quickly leave the area for your safety. Making your way down to Pirates Cove dock she handed each man a bag of coins. That should be enough for lodging and food and drinks while we are gone.

The six volunteers left the ship and climbed into the row boat. They made their way to the island. Skye could see they made it safely to shore and started climbing the hill with the launcher and smoke bombs in tow. Skye used her telescope to see when they reached the top of the hill. They gave the signal they were all set. Skye gave her crew orders to get ready to set sail at full speed. The crew hurried about preparing the ship. Scabbage signaled her they were ready. Skye's heart pounded as she gave the signal for the men to begin their attack on Hitchcock's ship.

As the sound of explosions echoed through the air, Skye prayed that their plan would work and they could make it past both King Neptune and the Queen's Navy to reach Mystic Island and claim their treasure. They made their way north up the coastline with Neptune's corner on their right side. Skye held her breath. They were at the edge of the island looking on their port side for Admiral Hitchcock's ship. As they sailed by Hitchcock's ship, it was completely covered with smoke. If you didn't know the ship was there, you couldn't see it. Skye was so happy her plan worked.

As they sailed towards Mystic Island, Skye stood at the helm, feeling the adrenaline pumping through her body. She couldn't wait to reach her treasure, and her excitement was palpable. Meanwhile, Gabriel watched her from a distance, torn between his feelings of betrayal and longing for her. He missed their conversations and meals together but couldn't bring himself to fully forgive her yet.

As they approached the coastline, Skye expertly steered the ship away from the treacherous rocks and towards the eastern southern tip of the island. Lowering the anchor, she quickly gathered her crew and instructed them to prepare provisions and weapons. She also reminded them to inform the professor to gather all necessary books and supplies.

After changing into more suitable clothes, Skye headed back onto the deck with her weapons in tow. As she surveyed her crew, she decided that a dozen men would be enough for their expedition. Spotting Patches among the sailors, she waved him over and gave him specific instructions for their landing on the island. She quickly approached him and asked if he wanted to join the treasure hunt or stay behind and man the ship. Patches eagerly replied, "I'd love to go on the quest! Rune can handle things here while I'm away." He added that they should also work on their weapons in case they come across any naval ships. Skye agreed with his plan and headed down to the galley to check on their supplies. Inside, she found Gabe assisting the chef with dinner preparations. The chef greeted her warmly, saying, "Captain, your supplies are nearly ready."

As Gabriel looked up at her, he smiled and said, "You know I'll be coming along to make sure you don't get into too much trouble." Skye playfully rolled her eyes but was secretly happy that he had decided to join the treasure hunt. She then went to check on the status of the boats they would be using to reach shore. The crew reported that they would be ready in about 30 minutes. Skye couldn't help but feel a surge of excitement - she loved going on treasure hunts and knew this one could potentially set them up for life. As she passed by the crew's cabin, one of the doors was open, and she saw Gabriel getting dressed inside. Memories of his muscular frame pressed against hers flooded back, and she couldn't help but stare for a moment. Suddenly, he turned and noticed her staring. Flustered, she quickly called out that they were leaving in 30 minutes before hurrying away.

On the other side of the closed door, Gabriel took a deep breath and leaned against it. His heart ached at the thought of being so close to Skye yet still feeling so far apart emotionally. He longed to hold her in his arms again but knew it wasn't possible - not until he forgave her for what had happened between them. He called out that he would be ready and prayed that they could put the past behind them on this treasure hunt. The two boats were fully stocked and ready to set sail for the treasure hunt. Skye held the coveted treasure map and the book containing the legend of the blue sapphire. The Professor, equipped with maps, languages, and gadgets, was on the other boat to help solve any puzzles they may encounter. As they landed on shore, Skye cautioned her crew to stay alert as they didn't know what dangers awaited them on this unknown island. Consulting the map, she directed her team toward their

first destination - the Druid Stones. The dense bush made it difficult for them to find a clear path, but Patches and Scabbage took the lead in clearing it for the rest of the group. Suddenly, Patches began screaming and pointing at something on his back. Upon closer inspection, Scabbage discovered it was just a harmless lizard. Despite being embarrassed, Patches couldn't help but laugh along with the rest of the group. But Skye quickly reminded them to focus and continue before it got dark.

Finally arriving at the ruins, Skye ordered Rocky and Frenchie to stand guard outside while she and the others entered the stones. In the center stood a circular stone with a dial containing various symbols - their next clue. Turning to Professor for guidance, he suddenly remembered that he hadn't paid attention to warnings written on their way in - "Once you enter, there is no turning back." Panic set in as they frantically searched for a way out, only to find all exits sealed with a mysterious force field. Skye angrily reprimanded the Professor for his negligence, but Gabriel came to his defense - it was an honest mistake, and he would surely figure out a solution. But time was running out, and they were trapped in these ruins until they could crack the puzzle. Gabriel grabbed Skye's arm and pulled her away from the group. "What were you thinking?" he whispered angrily. Skye could feel his grip tighten, his breath heavy with fear and frustration. She knew she had made a mistake, but it was an honest one. Skye should have been paying more attention to her surroundings. They would figure it out eventually; they always do. But for now, they were stuck in this druid force field with no way out.

As they sat on the cold stone floor, Skye noticed something peculiar. The symbols carved into the walls seemed to be fading and becoming harder to read. She grabbed a cloth and began wiping away the dirt and grime that covered them. Gabriel joined in, using his knife to carefully scrape away at the stubborn markings.

Meanwhile, the professor was hunched over his language parchments, muttering to himself as he tried to decipher their ancient meaning. Skye couldn't help but sneak glances at her treasure map and its intricate symbols, searching for any clues that could lead them out of this predicament.

Out of the corner of her eye, Skye saw skeletons scattered around the room, half-buried in the ground. She pointed them out to Gabriel and the professor and said, "If we don't solve this puzzle soon, we'll end up like those poor souls."

The pressure was mounting, and Skye could feel herself starting to panic. They needed to solve this before it was too late.

Just when she thought all hope was lost, Gabriel let out a triumphant laugh. "I know this language!" he exclaimed. "It's part of our Danish heritage with the Vikings." He explained how he had learned it in school and about the druids' belief in balance and energy.

Skye listened intently as Gabriel spoke, feeling a sense of relief wash over her. With his knowledge and her quick thinking, they could make it out of there alive.

Together, they carefully examined each of the eight stones, comparing them to the symbols in the professor's book. They had to get the order right or risk being trapped here forever. As they worked, Skye couldn't help but think about Gabriel's warning. She needed to be careful and not let greed or envy drive her actions. She vowed to keep her focus on finding a way out, no matter what sacrifices she may have to make

Skye looked at Gabriel with admiration and gratitude in her eyes. "We make a pretty good team when it comes to solving puzzles," she said with a smile.

Gabriel's finger traced over a series of symbols carved into the stone wall. "This one means warriors," he explained, pointing to an arrow-like shape pointing towards the sky. He continued to walk around, studying each symbol intently. There was one that resembled a capital R for journey and another that looked like a lightning bolt, which he remembered stood for wholeness. As he made his way down the row of symbols, Skye could see the excitement building in his eyes. Finally, he stopped at a symbol with a line running up and down with a triangle in the middle. "This one is the gateway," Gabriel announced triumphantly. "I know the eight symbols we need to use." He listed them off: Protection, Warrior, Opening, Flow, Movement, Journey, Breakthrough, and Gateway.

As they discussed the order in which to use them, Patches rolled his eyes and jokingly remarked about their group of pirates having trust issues. Skye bristled at his comment and asked if anyone else had doubts about joining her on this quest. To her surprise, it was Gabriel who stepped forward and offered his help. She couldn't help but ask why he would change his mind after all the past animosity between them. With a smile that made her heart skip a beat, Gabriel replied, "Because my heart tells me to." Skye felt herself blushing as she took in his gorgeous Caribbean blue eyes. Maybe this treasure hunt wouldn't be so bad after all. The captain's mouth hung open in shock, a rare sight for the fearless leader. She was speechless. The crew erupted into laughter at the miracle that had occurred on Mystic Island. Skye found her voice amongst the chaos and thanked Gabriel profusely. But he stopped her, stating his terms: after they retrieved the treasure, she must surrender herself and face the consequences of her actions. Skye hesitated, but Gabriel reminded her of their pirate customs - if she gave her word, she must keep it. He promised to speak on her behalf and explain that the destruction of his ship was an accident.

With a deep breath, Skye looked around at her crew and took Gabriel's hand, giving him her word. They would retrieve the treasure together and then return to face her sentence. As they began solving the puzzle of the symbol order, Skye noticed that one symbol seemed out of place. She pointed out to Gabriel that trust was essential in this step, so why did he eliminate the partnership symbol? After some discussion, they agreed that protection must also be important as it wouldn't be needed if they truly trusted each other.

Together, they carefully considered each of the remaining 8 symbols until they came up with a correct order. They started with the warrior symbol, which glowed when turned on the dial. Next was a journey, followed by movement and flow - all crucial elements for any adventure. The last four symbols were gateway, breakthrough, opening, and partnership. Guided by their intuition and reasoning, Gabriel and Skye selected Gateway as the next step in their journey.

As they turned the dial to the gateway, it began to glow, confirming their choice. With only three symbols left, they quickly decided on a breakthrough and opening before reaching the final symbol - partnership. They looked at each other with determination and turned the dial to reveal the glowing symbol. Finally, they had solved the puzzle and could proceed on their quest for treasure.

Gabriel's lips curved into a smile as he turned to Skye. "So far, so good," he said, "we're headed in the right direction." They approached the next symbol, labeled Breakthrough, and turned the knob to match it. The dial glowed once again, igniting a spark of excitement within Skye. They were getting closer. The final two clues were Opening and Partnership. Skye surmised they needed to open something together. "It must be the partnership symbol," she declared. Gabriel nodded in agreement and they turned the dial to that symbol, but nothing happened. Disappointment washed over them as Skye realized she was wrong and Gabriel's suggestion of Protection was correct. Suddenly, the dial began glowing brighter and brighter until a blinding light shot up into the sky, causing the earth to tremble. Then, silence fell upon the group as they listened to birds chirping in the distance.

Skye marched over to her guards at the entrance of the opening and barked orders. They snapped to attention and replied with a crisp "Yes, captain." Skye couldn't help but feel pleased that they had solved another piece of the riddle and were one step closer to finding the treasure. She then shared her plan with her crew - they needed to go back to their ship and sail to the northern-eastern point of the island. Rocky protested, reminding Skye that they would have to pass by Mermaid Island, where their enticing songs lured men to their deaths. Skye thanked him for bringing this up and instructed her chef to retrieve a box hidden in her quarters as well as an Astrolabe, which would help them navigate close to Mystic Island's shoreline away from mermaid island's deadly trap.

As her crew set off on their task, Skye turned to face the group and asked if they were ready for the next step in their treasure hunt. Each member nodded in determination, and they left the druid stone circle. Skye consulted the treasure map, which led them down a winding pathway to the entrance of a cave. They walked cautiously, their senses on high alert. Suddenly, Skye held up her fist, signaling for everyone to stop as she heard a rustling in the bushes ahead. She motioned for Patches and Eric to scout it out while pointing Scabbage and Gabriel in the opposite direction. The professor...

Skye and her crew followed their professor, swords clutched tightly in their hands as they made their way down the overgrown path.

Suddenly, a flurry of arrows flew towards them, one grazing Whitty's arm. They quickly dove into nearby bushes for cover, hearing the sounds of fighting in the distance. Skye's heart raced with worry for Gabriel as they waited in tense silence. Minutes passed, feeling like hours, until finally, Scabbage and Gabriel emerged from the brush. Patches and Eric appeared from the opposite direction, accompanied by two tribesmen. Patches shrugged helplessly, admitting he didn't understand their language or why they were attacking. The professor stepped forward, studying their attire with its face tattoos and weapons before declaring that they were from the Soulfire tribe, protectors of the island against intruders. He tried to communicate with them in their native tongue, and they responded eagerly.

When Skye asked what they said, the professor relayed that they were on sacred ground and needed to leave immediately. But Skye refused to back down; she told the professor to ask if they would show them where the cave entrance was and promised to reward them with food and water. One warrior agreed while his companion cowered in fear. Patches suggested tying him up but Skye reminded him to just use a basic knot.

As they continued following Garlic (the name the professor had discovered), he also learned that he and his tribe were descendants of the Aztecs. The path grew narrower as they walked along the side of the mountain, forced to single file through dense bushes. Gabriel whispered to Skye, questioning whether Garlic could be leading them into danger. She reassured him that according to the professor when Aztecs gave their word, they kept it. Interrupting their conversation, the professor announced that Garlic had revealed that they were getting close. And as they pushed through thick bushes, Skye could see that they were indeed nearing their goal. The professor's voice echoed through the dense foliage as he shouted, "Garlic said we're getting close!" They emerged from the thick bushes and came upon a clearing with a large dirt patch in front of them. Garlic pointed to the bushes and said something in his native language. The professor translated, "He says we must cut back this bush to reach the entrance of the cave." Skye nodded and exclaimed, "Let's get to work, men. We're getting closer to our treasure." With swords in hand, they hacked away at the bushes until they were able to see the cave entrance.

After several hours of hard work, Skye suggested they rest and replenish their energy before entering the dark cave. She sat down near the edge of the clearing and gazed out at the sun setting over the horizon. Gabriel noticed her eyes starting to droop and gently shook her awake when it was time to continue their journey. As they prepared to enter the cave, Garlic surprised them by saying he wanted to join their quest.

Skye welcomed him, knowing that his tribe had been guarding the treasure for centuries and could provide valuable insight. With their torches lit, they descended into the cave and came across a stone bridge with ancient Aztec symbols engraved on each step. There was also a warning written in an unknown language just before the bridge. Skye turned to the professor and asked if he knew what it meant. He studied the writing carefully before translating, "It says that only those who follow the rulers of light will find their way through this darkness. Those who succumb to darkness will meet their fate." Skye groaned at yet another riddle in their path. Gabriel walked over to her and took her hands in his, reminding her to think outside the box and use her intelligence to solve the puzzle. Patches was exploring around the area when he accidentally stepped back onto one of the stones on the bridge. To everyone's surprise, the stone lit up and glowed, illuminating their path forward. Professor, in one of your books, do you have a list of the Aztec sun gods? The professor got very excited and exclaimed I do let me find it. The professor found the book and opened it up to find the numerous pictures of the sun gods that the Aztec people worship. Skye became very excited, studied the symbols, and said to the group we must only step on the Aztec sun god symbols; otherwise, the stone you are on will collapse, so we will go in a single file line. The bridge had three symbols across on each row; they were 6 feet by six feet. Skye studied the symbols, then referenced the book and began stepping on the stones. First row was easy since Patches stepped on one of the stones with only two to choose from. The professor brought the book near the bridge. He said the book is showing 20 different Aztec gods. We just have to match their symbols and what their god power was. Skye asked to see the book she studied and found a photo of a god named Quetzalcoati that matched the drawing. Garlic started to walk on it and Skye stopped him. Wait, it says that God was a feathered serpent and god of death and resurrection, so not a sun god. This one in the corner's name is Chantico, and was considered a sun god. Skye said I will go first in case we are wrong in our theory Gabriel said I will go with you. They held hands and stepped on the stone, and it started to glow. They waited for the stone to collapse. Nothing happened. Skye sighed good, and we picked the correct stone.

They came to the next set of stones. They laid the book on the stone and found the three different gods: Ehecal, Xipetitec, and Huitzllopachil. The first one is the god of rain, the second is agriculture, and the third one is the sun. They picked up the book, held hands, and stepped onto the next stone. It glowed and remained glowing as if lighting the path for them to follow. Skye still held her breath as I was near racking. They were now standing in front of the third row; the professor and Garlic were standing on the stone behind them. Skye opened the book and immediately saw the middle stone symbol. It was Tonatiuh, and he said he was the sun god that allowed the sun to come up on the east and go down on the west. Skye and Gabriel held hands again and stepped onto the stone. It also glowed.

Whitty and Skip were getting so excited. Now, they were standing in front of the fourth row. They were halfway there. Patches and Eric moved onto the first stone. Scabbage was on the second stone. Scar and Whittey were the last ones to step on the bridge. Skye opened the book again, and her eyes were drawn to the middle god she found in the book. She was a Coyolxauhqui moon goddess, so it wasn't that one. The one on the left name was Tlahuizcalponte also known as the god of the dawn and a sun god. They stepped onto the stone, and it glowed as the path was getting brighter and brighter, with sweat dripping down their faces.

Skye and Gabriel were looking at the last row, and Skye could feel her heart racing. They looked at each other and then at the last three stones. They looked at the book again to find the last three matching pictures. The one in the left corner was Mictlantecuhtli; they found he was known as the god of death, so they eliminated that stone only two left. The one in the middle was Telopolollot, known as the god of animals and earthquakes. Skye started to take the right step Gabriel said wait to look at what it says. The last one was Chalchiuhtlicue, which said that her name means "Lady of the jade skirts." She was the goddess of water. Skye was shocked and looked at Gabriel. We got this far, and one God is a death god; the next one is animals and earthquakes, and the last one is a water god. Which do we pick? She heard Scabbage yell, "What's the hold-up."

She yelled back, "Don't rush us." Gabriel was still reading the book, trying to find more information.

Gabriel shouted. "I found it; it says even though she was a water goddess, she was considered a sun god,"

Skye said, "Alright, let's go."

They took each other's hands and stepped on the stone as the path was complete. They stepped off the bridge to the other side. There was a sign similar to the one at the druid circle saying there is no going back, only forward. Gabriel and Skye looked at each other and realized that the bridge was going to collapse. They started shouting to get off the bridge as fast as they could. Skip and Whittey noticed the stones behind them were crumbling, looked at each other, and said at the same time run. Skye and Gabriel helped the professor and Garlic off the bridge. The others were running as fast as they could. Patches and Eric made Gabriel help them off the bridge. Scabbage was running as fast as he could. Gabriel said, "For a big man he does have speed."

As the bridge kept lowering, Skye started to panic and shouted at Scar and Whittey to run faster, or they wouldn't make it. Scar ran as if their lives depended on it, which they did. They made it to the last stone and jumped to reach the edge. Whittey quickly stepped off just as the last step disappeared, but Skip started plummeting downward. Scabbage's reflexes kicked in, and he grabbed Skip's arm and pulled him back to safety. Skye let out a sigh of relief as everyone was now safe, and they could move on with the treasure hunt. Skye said, "Okay, everyone, look around and be careful; there are booby traps everywhere."

Patches noticed a pathway off to the side and pointed it out to the group. Skye reminded everyone to be on high alert for traps as they followed Patches' lead. Skye took charge and led the way, stopping abruptly when she spotted a good-sized rock. With precision, she threw it ahead of them, and poisonous arrows shot out across the path. She signaled for everyone to hold up as she repeated the process with a few more rocks. When no arrows came out, Skye said she would go first to make sure it was safe.

With caution, Skye moved aside some cobwebs blocking their path and revealed what appeared to be a tunnel. On the ground were stones with Xs and Os etched onto them. Skye couldn't help but think how strange it was that they resembled a game of tic tac toe. Gabriel approached her and inspected the stones before exclaiming, "Tic tac toe!"

Gabriel stood next to Skye, their eyes fixed on the ancient stones as they contemplated a game of tic tac toe. The professor joined them, explaining the game's history while they discussed their strategies. Gabriel, confident in his skills from playing with his father during long trips, made the first move and placed an X on the top left square. As they waited for the O to make its move, Skye reassured Gabriel that his memories would return in time.

Just as they were about to continue the game, one of the O's suddenly started moving and landed in the top right corner. With this unexpected turn, Gabriel quickly countered by placing another X in the middle square, blocking the O from making three in a row. Skye eagerly watched as the O spun before landing on the right middle square.

Feeling triumphant, Gabriel moved his final X to the bottom right corner and declared himself the winner. However, their celebration was cut short as the ground beneath them began shaking violently. Without hesitation, they both screamed, "RUN!" and took off towards safety.

As they continued to run, boulders started falling behind them. In between gasps for air, Gabriel couldn't help but taunt that he won fair and square. But their focus remained on outrunning the danger until they were finally safe.

The group ran through the winding paths of the ancient ruins, their hearts pounding and lungs burning. They finally reached a gap in the path, four feet across, with boulders chasing them from behind. Skye shouted that they needed to change it, and they all sprinted forward, taking a daring leap and landing on the other side. One by one, they crossed over as the boulders crashed down into the ravine below. Gabriel remarked that he shuddered to think what would have happened if they had lost.

As they caught their breath, Skye shone her torch ahead and saw sixteen square stones arranged in a grid of four by four. Each stone had an intricate Egyptian symbol carved into it. It seemed like some kind of safe, and they would need to decipher the symbols and input the correct code to open it. Above the stones, there was a clue on how to solve the puzzle.

Skye called the professor over, who rummaged through his bag of books. However, he couldn't find the specific hieroglyphics book they needed for this puzzle. Skye became frustrated, realizing that they had traveled all this way only to be unable to solve the final piece because of a dropped book.

She started getting angry at the professor, but Gabriel intervened and calmed her down. He suggested that they could still figure it out without the book since they had solved all the previous puzzles successfully. Turning to the professor, he asked if any of the symbols seemed familiar.

The professor examined the 16 symbols closely and recognized two as gods named Horus and Osiris. He also identified another symbol as an ankh, which represented a god or deity. However, he didn't recognize any of the other symbols.

The three of them stood there, trying to make sense of the symbols and their order while looking for four specific ones to input into the lock. If they chose incorrectly, the symbols would crumble, and they would meet a terrible fate. Skye grew more frustrated, questioning how they could come so far only to be defeated by the final puzzle.

Gabriel stepped closer to her, wrapping his arm around her in comfort and speaking softly. He assured her that they would figure it out and suggested that they backtrack to look for the missing book.

Gabriel's arm wrapped around Skye, offering her warmth and comfort. She could feel his steady breath on her neck as he spoke in a hushed tone. "We'll figure it out," he said, suggesting they take a break and replenish their energy before tackling the problem again. Skye nodded, feeling drained from hours of searching for answers. They made makeshift beds and shared a meal and some water, with a splash of rum to ease their nerves. As they rested, Skye surveyed their surroundings - a dimly lit cave with a cool breeze coming from the west and the sound of rushing water to the south. The wall torches were positioned to the right of her, which she determined was east based on her compass. Suddenly, Skye exclaimed, "I think I know what the elements in the scripture are!" Gabriel was intrigued and asked for more information.

"Air, earth, water, and fire - those must be the elements referenced in the stones," Skye explained. But then she remembered that they had lost the book with the symbols that would help them decipher which element each stone represented. The professor sighed sadly at their misfortune, but Skye remained determined. Patches suddenly chimed in, asking why they couldn't just use the symbols to solve the puzzle. Confused, Skye and her companions turned to Patches and admitted that they were clueless about the symbols' meanings. Patches scratched his head before realizing that he had grown up with his father, who was an expert in this area. In fact, he knew all of the symbol meanings by heart. Excitedly, Patches began explaining each symbol and its corresponding element to the group.

As Patches and Skye stood in the dark cave, surrounded by ancient hieroglyphics, the professor asked Patches to explain the symbols. He confidently pointed out Osiris, Horus, and Ankh- symbols of gods- and a spiral rectangle representing shelter. Skye's excitement grew as she connected these symbols to elements they had already found on Earth. Patches identified the symbol for fire - an upside down heart with flames shooting out - and air - a cursive 3 with three lines next to it. Skye was elated at having discovered three of the four elements they needed to open the door in front of them. However, their attempts to move the stones towards the door were unsuccessful. Skye attempted to pry one out with a knife but even Patches couldn't budge them. As Skye paced, trying to think of a solution, Gabriel walked over and jokingly asked if he was interrupting something. Skye shook her head, frustrated that they were so close yet still unable to unlock the door. Skye glanced at Gabriel, her worry lines etched deep in her forehead. "I'm just trying to figure out this riddle," she whispered, holding the clue in one hand and rubbing her temples with the other.

Gabriel wrapped his arms around her, pulling her close. "Don't worry," he reassured her. "We've come this far. We won't be defeated." Skye's eyes shifted over to Patches, who stood in front of the stones, panting heavily. He took a big gulp from his water sash, some of it spilling onto the stones below. Skye noticed that the waterstone seemed to react to the liquid.

Without hesitation, she ran over to Patches and snatched the water sash from his mouth. "If you wanted some, all you had to do was ask," Patches joked as Skye carefully poured more water onto the stone. Suddenly, it started to loosen from its surroundings.

Excitedly, Skye grabbed hold of the stone and removed it from its place. She and Gabriel cheered at the same time.

"We need elements like water for the water stone, air for air, fire for fire," they said in unison. They brought a torch closer to the firestone, and it began to move and loosen. Gabriel quickly grabbed it and placed it next to the waterstone.

"Eric!" Skye shouted. "Bring me a blanket so I can make air."

Gabriel grabbed the blanket and started fanning the air stone until it came loose enough for Skye to retrieve it. Now they had three stones, only one left.

The professor chimed in, "But how are we going to get the earthstone? It's sitting on top of the earth."

Skye smiled confidently. "The stone may be stationary, but we can use dirt to loosen it." Gabriel wasted no time, grabbing a handful of dirt and rubbing it onto the earth stone until it became free.

Skye jumped up and down with excitement while Gabriel hugged her tightly. They gathered all four stones and placed them in front of the door, examining the four openings above.

"How do we know which stones go where?" Gabriel asked.

"It matters," Patches interjected. "I remember all my digs with my father. Nothing was simple; everything had order and a purpose."

Skye added, "We'll figure it out. We're so close to unlocking the treasure on the other side of this door." She looked up at the door again and noticed a small compass in the upper right corner with N, S, W, and E marked on it. Skye slapped her forehead. "Of course!" she exclaimed. "We need to put the stones in the vault in the correct order."

"I remember feeling a strong gust of air coming from the west," Skye recalled as she picked up the air stone. She put the stone on the west side.

The smooth, polished stone fit perfectly into the wall, almost as if it had been waiting to be placed there. Gabriel checked his notes and confidently directed the group toward the torches on the right side of the room. With a grunt, he lifted a heavy stone with a fiery symbol and placed it in the designated spot on the right side of the circular pattern on the floor. It seamlessly merged into the wall.

Skye's heart raced with excitement as Gabriel addressed the remaining two stones. She looked down and saw dirt representing the earth on the ground below her feet. As Gabriel reached for the tile with an earth symbol, Skye suddenly stopped him. "Wait!" she cried out, her eyes fixated on the ground behind them. "Can you hear that? The sound of running water?" Everyone fell silent and listened as the faint sound of a river could be heard in the distance. Skye's mind raced as she realized that water should go to the bottom, not the earth.

With shaking hands, she carefully picked up the stone with a water symbol and placed it in the bottom slot. It, too, merged smoothly into the wall. The group stepped back, holding their breath in anticipation of what would happen next.

Suddenly, the ground began to shake violently, causing everyone to stumble and grab onto each other for support. A blinding light illuminated from the center top of the door and traveled down to meet each cornerstone, creating a golden line that connected them all. With one last jolt, the ground stopped shaking, and the door slowly opened inwards.

As they cautiously entered through the now open doorway, Skye searched for any source of light in the darkness ahead. Her torch revealed oil lamps scattered throughout the room, casting flickering shadows on ancient artifacts lining the walls. With a quick flick of her torch, Skye lit one of these lamps and watched as it spread a warm glow throughout the space.

As they entered the dimly lit room, Skye's eyes widened in amazement at the sight before her. The walls were lined with glittering treasures from various ancient civilizations - crowns, necklaces, and other priceless artifacts filled every nook and cranny. But amidst all this wealth, she couldn't spot the one thing they had come for - the elusive Sapphire stone.

She turned to the Professor, her trusted friend, and asked about the stone's whereabouts. He shrugged and pointed to a sign that read, "Beware of greed; it can destroy you." Skye knew they had to stay focused or risk getting lost in their desire for riches.

That's when she noticed six large crates placed strategically around the room. Each crate represented a different time period - Egyptian, Greek, Roman, Mayan, Mesopotamian, and Druids. And they seemed to fit together like puzzle pieces.

With Gabriel by her side, she climbed the stairs to get a better view. As they looked down at the treasure laid out below them, Skye couldn't shake the feeling that something was off. She instructed Scabbage and Patches to move the Egyptian crate toward the Mesopotamian one while Professor Eric and his assistant moved the Mesopotamian crate toward them. With a few pushes and shoves, the two crates clicked together perfectly.

Garlic, their native guide, joined them and helped push the Mayan crate toward the others while Gabriel moved the Druid treasure next to it. As each crate locked into place with a satisfying click, Skye urged them to line up the last two crates - Greek and Roman - and push them together.

Once all six pieces were connected, Skye could sense they were almost there. She gathered her crewmates- Patches, Scabbage, and Gabriel - on one side while Skipper and Eric stood ready on the other. With a unified effort, they pushed the pieces together until they formed one giant crate.

Suddenly, the ground trembled and split open to reveal a grand staircase leading up to a platform where the shining Sapphire stone sat. Skye couldn't believe their luck and ran towards it with excitement, eager to claim the treasure that had eluded them for so long.

Skye's heart raced with excitement as she sprinted towards the steps of the ancient temple. She could see a giant scale next to the steps, its intricate carvings gleaming in the sunlight.

As they approached, Skye noticed writing on each step that read, "This is the scale of faith and trust you must work together to receive your treasure. Beware, if you answer the question incorrectly, you will meet your fate." The group turned to the Professor, seeking guidance.

He studied the writings and explained, "Two people must go up the steps on either side at the same time and will be asked a question. There are four in total, and each one must be answered correctly, or the next step will get higher." You must fully trust one another, or it won't work.

Gabriel stepped forward, taking Skye's hand in his. "We can do this," he said confidently. "We've come too far to give up now."

Skye was hesitant, unsure if they should risk it. She spoke softly to Gabriel, confessing her doubts about their trust in each other after all that had happened between them. But Gabriel looked deep into her eyes and declared his love for her. Skye couldn't help but tear up as she grabbed his face and kissed him passionately.

Patches' voice broke through their moment, making a joke about not wanting to see any more public displays of affection. They all laughed as Gabriel and Skye stepped onto the bottom step and signaled to the Professor that they were ready.

The professor read the first question aloud: "Do you trust one another completely?" At the same time, Skye and Gabriel both answered with a resounding "Yes". The stone beneath them began moving upwards, signaling their correct response.

They reached the next step, where the Professor asked, "Do you believe in one another?" Again, they answered in unison with a confident "yes", and the stone lifted them up further.

As they approached the third question, Skye couldn't help but make a snarky comment about it being ancient wedding vows. But when Professor asked if they loved each other with all their hearts, Skye's heart overflowed with emotion as she looked at Gabriel and said, "Yes".

Gabriel and Skye stood on either side of a grand staircase, their eyes fixed on the towering platform above them where the legendary Sapphire Stone was said to be kept. They had answered three previous questions correctly, and each step they took brought them closer to their ultimate goal. As they stepped onto the fourth and final step, the professor's voice boomed through the room, warning them of the difficulty of the last question. Skye yelled down, asking why he was shaking his head. The professor replied that she wouldn't like the next question. Skye scoffed, confident in her love for treasure and determination to fulfill her father's dying wish.

But as the professor posed the final question - "Do you put this person before your treasures?" - Skye's mood shifted from brash confidence to frustration and doubt. She stomped her feet on the small step she stood on, muttering to herself about how unfair it all was. However, Gabriel spoke up in a calm voice, reminding her of her kind heart and selflessness towards her crew and their island community. At his words, Skye's eyes welled up with unexpected emotion.

Despite her tough exterior as a pirate captain, she couldn't deny the truth in Gabriel's words. She wiped away her tears and shouted down to the professor that she was ready for the final question. Alongside Gabriel, she confidently answered "yes" when asked if she would put this person before all riches.

The steps started moving upwards towards the platform, and with each passing moment, Skye's anticipation grew. As they reached the top and walked towards the glistening Sapphire Stone, she couldn't help but give a smug laugh at Gabriel's earlier doubt about her priorities. But underneath that laughter was a deep sense of gratitude for his unwavering belief in her.

All around them, their crewmates Scabbage, Patches, Skipper, and Eric had stopped dancing around with their own treasures and were watching in anticipation. Patches whispered to the others about how they knew Skye and her love for treasure. They all had a scar or two from trying to take something she claimed as her own.

But they also knew the true nature of their captain and how she had been under a witch's spell, obsessed with treasure, before they found a way to break it. They were grateful they wouldn't have to cross paths with that side of her again.

As the professor finally asked the last question - "Do you put this person before all riches?" - both Skye and Gabriel confidently answered, "Yes." And with that, the Sapphire Stone was theirs, a symbol of their bond and mutual trust. As they shared a victorious smile, Skye couldn't help but think about how lucky she was to have someone like Gabriel by her side.

Gabriel let out a hearty laugh, "You never know," he said with a playful wink. Skye's gaze was fixated on the magnificent blue sapphire, about six inches tall and three inches in diameter, sparkling in the sunlight. Patches yelled up from below, warning her to be careful and not unleash any curses while handling the powerful stone. Skye rolled her eyes and retorted sarcastically, "Ha ha, very funny." She made sure to carefully inspect the area around the stone for any hidden dangers, such as deadly scorpions or spiders.

As she looked at the etching in front of the sapphire, it read "Remember your wish must be selfless or pay the consequences." Skye cautiously picked up the stone and held it out for everyone to see. Gabriel asked if he could hold it, but before she could respond, Skye grabbed her sword and swung it toward him, yelling, "No! It's all mine! I'll kill you!" The look of horror on his face was priceless, and Skye couldn't help but burst into laughter. She then handed Gabriel the stone and announced that she was going to explore the treasures on this landing.

The treasures were unlike anything Skye had ever seen before. There were old-looking swords of various kinds, staffs of all sizes and shapes, and different types of tridents. She wondered if Neptune's trident or Poseidon's trident were among them. As she continued to search, she spotted Neptune's trident among the others. Legend says that Neptune lost his trident during a great battle under the sea against Poseidon and Jaserula, Queen of the Mermaids. The gods above intervened and took away their tridents, banishing them to different parts of the ocean where they must remain.

Skye grabbed Neptune's trident with excitement and then noticed something else out of the corner of her eye - Ursula's trident. She searched for Poseidon's trident and finally found it buried under some rocks. Skye couldn't believe her luck and decided to keep the tridents as leverage in case she ever needed them. As she moved aside more rocks, she uncovered what appeared to be a hidden step. She eagerly cleared away more debris, wondering where it would lead her. Skye approached the opening in the cave, her heart racing with adrenaline. She called out to Gabriel, who was still at the top, and told him she was going to explore the steps leading down. "Okay," he shouted back, "I'll look for a way out."

As she descended, Skye could feel the air becoming heavier and more humid. The walls of the staircase were damp and slick under her palms. She reached the bottom and found herself in a treasure vault filled with jewels and gold.

"Grab anything you can!" she yelled to her crewmates above. "We have to leave before this place collapses!"

But as she made her way back up to the entrance, she realized that Gabriel and the sapphire stone were missing. Skye's blood boiled as she cursed him for being a traitor and promised to hunt him down. Skye started yelling you murderous trait, I will hunt you down and kill you.

Suddenly, Gabriel appeared from behind some rocks and asked what all the commotion was about. Skye accused him of stealing their treasure, but he protested his innocence and said he had left to find a way out. Gabriel told her he found a way out and to follow him. She shouted at her men to come up the stairs. Gabriel had found a way out. The men all came up carrying as much treasure as possible. The ground started shaking, and Skye said to run. The treasure is collapsing inward. They looked down and could see the treasures starting to move. They started spinning in a circle. Skye said, quickly follow Gabriel. Gabriel showed them the opening he had found that leads to the outside of the mountain.

They quickly gathered their loot and followed Gabriel down a narrow path along the side of the mountain. Patches saved Scabbage from slipping off the edge, and joked about needing rum as payment. They made their way down the small edge on the side of the mountain.

The path widened as they neared the beach, where their ship was waiting for them. As they waited for their crewmates to lower the boats, Skye thanked Gabriel for joining her on this adventure. He replied with a mischievous smile and a promise to collect his repayment in her cabin.

Their moment was interrupted by Patches' teasing and the arrival of their fellow pirates. Skye showed them some of the treasures they had acquired and asked Rune if Chef had retrieved the item from her cabin. Rune said yes. They rowed back to her ship, Vixen, with all their loot. Skye had the blue sapphire securely in her sash and the three Tridents.

As they sailed away from danger, Skye couldn't help but wonder about Captain Barrack from the queen's Navy. Her crew assured her that they had lost their pursuers, but Skye couldn't shake the feeling that they would need to be on guard.

The crew scurried around, hoisting heavy chests onto the deck of the ship. Captain Skye stood at the helm, a victorious smile on her face as she watched her men load their latest treasures. "Hip, hip, hooray for Captain Skye!" they cheered, their voices carrying across the open sea.

Skye barked orders for the treasure to be brought below deck and divided among the crew. As the men carried out her commands, she retreated to her cabin, clutching the coveted tritons, crown, and Sapphire stone. She instructed them to steer toward Mermaid Island while staying close to the Mystic Island coastline. The crew exchanged worried glances – they had all heard tales of sailors falling under the spell of mermaids' enchanting songs and drowning in pursuit of them.

But Skye assured them not to worry. "I have a safety net if we encounter them," she said confidently. Her crew trusted her with their lives and knew she wouldn't lead them into danger.

As Skye entered her cabin, she noticed the door was slightly ajar. Instinctively, she drew her sword and cautiously stepped inside. To her surprise, she found Gabriel pouring glasses of rum. "I thought we were past that," he said with a smirk, gesturing to his unarmed state.

Skye couldn't help but laugh at herself for being so paranoid. She put away her sword and accepted the drink from Gabriel. But then he mentioned something about payment owed to him and Skye's mind immediately went to the deal she made to return to his kingdom and turn herself in.

But Gabriel clarified that he wasn't referring to that kind of payment. "You have way too many clothes on to start the repayment," he said with a mischievous grin.

Skye giggled and quickly shed her clothes, as did Gabriel. They embraced each other passionately, their bodies entwined as they gave in to their desires. Afterward, they lay in the afterglow, not saying a word but simply enjoying the bliss of being together.

Gabriel broke the silence with a question about the necklace Skye always wore around her neck – a small glass vial filled with liquid. Skye explained that it was a reminder of her past and all the struggles she had overcome. Gabriel smiled and kissed her, grateful to have Skye by his side once again.

The delicate glass, filled with shimmering liquid, rested in Skye's hand. She explained to Gabriel that it was a gift from an old lover - mermaid tears - and she had promised to never take it off. There was a knock on the cabin door, interrupting their conversation. Skye reluctantly left the bed as Gabriel tried to stop her, reminding her of her captain duties. She smiled and replied that they were nearing Mermaid Island and she needed to get ready. After quickly grabbing her robe and putting it on, she told the visitor to enter.

It was Chef, carrying a tray of food. Skye jumped up to give him a hug, grateful for his safe return with both her life and treasure. Chef expressed how much he worries about her, and Skye replied that he is like a second father to her. She thanked him for bringing food, as she was starving. Looking over at Gabriel, Chef reassured him that there was enough for both of them despite being on a small ship.

As soon as Chef's face turned serious, Skye knew what he was going to say. He spoke softly to her, asking if she was sure about using the horn. They both know that the woman who wants it hasn't forgiven Skye yet. Skye confidently stated that it was the only way to safely pass by her territory during their treasure hunt. She had something that this mermaid had been searching for centuries and would use it as leverage. Chef asked what did you find? Skye explained about the Trident she had found and knew mermaids would want it back. Chef agreed he felt better.

After the Chef left, Gabriel asked Skye who this woman was and why she hates you. Skye replied by saying it was a long story and they didn't have time for details right now. Gabriel agreed although he didn't fully understand the situation.

Skye quickly dressed and grabbed the trident and horn before heading up to the upper deck. As they neared Mermaid Cove, she could hear their enchanting song growing louder. She summoned Patches and Scabbage to go below deck and bring her some supplies.

Skye brushed her fingers against the smooth trident and rough, curved horn on her belt. She could hear the faint melody of mermaids singing as she climbed up to the upper deck. "Patches, Scabbage!" she called out. The two sailors scurried to her side. "Go below deck and fetch candles for the crew," Skye commanded. Patches raised an eyebrow. "Captain, is this really the best time for...romantic endeavors?" he asked, trying to suppress a grin. Skye shot him a withering glare. "You idiot," she hissed. "The wax is for their ears, to block out the siren's call." Patches apologized and dashed off with Scabbage.

Standing at the edge of the ship, Skye surveyed the ocean and her crew. So far, no one seemed to be affected by the mermaid's song. Gabriel joined her at the railings. "We'll get through this, just like we've been through so much already," he said with a chuckle, recalling their tumultuous history together.

Scabbage and Patches returned with the candles. Skye instructed her crew to put them in their ears to block out the alluring voices of the mermaids. "But how will we communicate?" Eric shouted from the crow's nest. Skye raised her voice over the din of waves and wind."We've sailed together for years; everyone knows their roles and responsibilities. We just need to trust each other." She also reminded them to use hand signals if necessary and that she could still hear them.

As they neared Mermaid Cove, a thick fog descended upon them, obscuring their vision. Skye knew this was just the beginning; soon, her men would fall under Jaserela's spell and be lured to their deaths by her enchanted song.

Skye remembered the legend of Jaserela, a mermaid who fell in love with a sailor and wanted him to join her in the sea. But he chose to remain human, breaking her heart and earning her eternal ire. Skye's own tumultuous relationship with Jaserela only added fuel to the fire.

The siren's song grew louder and more intense as if all the mermaids were singing together. This was unusual, as they usually disapproved of Jaserela's destructive ways.

As they approached the end of Mermaid Island, Skye could see her crew starting to fall under the spell. Their eyes become glassy and distant, a sign that they were being hypnotized. She couldn't risk losing any of them, so she took out her horn and blew into it with all her might. The high-pitched sound cut through the air like a soprano opera singer's voice, shattering some of the enchantment. For now, at least, they were safe from the siren's call.

As the sirens' song faded, Skye could feel her heart racing and her palms sweating. She reached for the horn again, blowing as hard as she could until, finally, the sound stopped and she shouted "Drop anchor!". Turning to Gabriel, Skye announced, "I have to go speak to her. I'll need some things from my cabin first." With determination in her eyes, Skye grabbed a leather bag and filled it with a mermaid trident and a lost mermaid ruler's crown that she had retrieved from a treasure vault. Gabriel, concerned for her safety, insisted on accompanying her. As they made their way to the boat, he noticed a gold locket on Skye's desk. It seemed strangely familiar to him, but he didn't want to pry at the moment.

Once they were on the water, Skye directed Gabriel towards a clearing where Jaserula, with her long raven hair and enchanting emerald eyes, was waiting for them. Her beautiful tail shimmered with silver specks and hints of gold and pink. As Gabriel stood speechless at the sight of her, Skye greeted Jaserula with familiarity. However, there was an undercurrent of anger in Jaserula's voice as she accused Skye of interfering with sailors who dared enter her domain. Standing tall and confident, Skye responded by offering a deal to spare her crew from Jaserula's deadly grasp.

Jaserela's voice growled with frustration as she demanded, "What could you possibly have that I want?" She glared at Gabriel before turning her attention back to Skye.

"Well, he is quite handsome," Jaserela said with a sly smile, "but don't worry, I won't try to steal him away from you."

Skye quickly interjected, "No, no, he's not-" but Jaserela cut her off with a dismissive wave of her hand. "I'm not interested in him like that. But I am interested in what you have in your possession."

Curiosity piqued, Skye reached into her bag and pulled out a gleaming mermaid trident adorned with ancient symbols. Jaserela gasped and tried to grab it, but Skye held it out of reach and said carefully, "Not so fast. How did you even find this? It's been lost for centuries after the great battle under the sea."

Excitement bubbled within Jaserela as she exclaimed, "Do you know what this means? We can rebuild our home again and live under the sea once more!"

But Skye's response was hesitant: "How can I trust you after what you did to me?"

Anger flickered in Jaserela's eyes as she retorted, "After you betrayed me! I saved your life", said Skye.

Jaserula turns to Gabriel; she asks sarcastically, "Did she ever tell you how we first met and what we meant to each other?"

Gabriel shook his head in confusion and replied honestly, "I didn't even know you two had a history until a few moments ago."

A wicked smile spread across Jaserela's lips as she decided it was time to reveal the truth. But before she could continue, Skye urgently interrupted: "We don't have time for this. Let's just make our deal and be on our way."

But Jaserela was not easily swayed. "I rarely have visitors," she said with a sly grin. "I think I'll tell my tale first, then you can leave." With a dramatic flourish, Jaserela began her story and explained to Gabriel the mermaid's tradition of walking on land every 50 years for 6 weeks in search of love. She recounted how she had met Skye in a small town near Barbados, mesmerized by her beauty and adventurous spirit.

As Jaserela spoke, Gabriel couldn't help but interrupt his own memories of meeting Skye and feeling the same way. Irritated, Jaserela snarled at him to let her finish her story. She continued, describing their conversation at a local saloon and how they had both shared tales of their travels while enjoying ale together. Jaserela's heart fluttered as she remembered the warmth of Skye's hand in hers and the excitement she felt when Skye invited her back to her rented room.

She held me close, her soft skin and gentle touch sending shivers down my spine. We lost ourselves in each other, our bodies moving in perfect harmony as the passion consumed us. Outside, the sun set and rose again, as we couldn't bear to break apart for too long. Eventually, I mustered up the courage to reveal my true form as a mermaid, explaining that I was only on land to find a mate before returning to the sea. Skye was shocked but remained calm, deciding to make the most of our limited time together. As the weeks passed, our love grew deeper and stronger, but I couldn't help but hope that she would join me in the ocean. But as my departure neared, I asked her if she had made a decision yet. Syke said she was still undecided and would tell me in the morning. In the morning, I woke up to an empty room and a broken heart as she had left without a word. Crushed, I returned to the sea with tears in my eyes.

Gabriel asked about the horn Skye used to call for me, and Jaserula explained that it was a gift of love from me to her, a tradition among mermaids to ensure we can always find our beloved ones no matter where they are. He then asked about the tears she wore around her neck. Jaserula explained they were shed by me as I left the land heartbroken and eventually got caught in a fisherman's net. My heart was heavy, and my surroundings blurred as tears threatened to fall. Suddenly, I was tangled in a fisherman's net, struggling to free myself. The man who had caught me shouted with excitement, declaring himself rich for catching a mermaid.

Just when I thought all hope was lost, Skye's ship appeared, and the Vixen came alongside the fisherman's boat. Skye came abroad, swords blazing, and cut me loose from the net. She had saved my life once again. Overcome with emotion, I couldn't help but cry in gratitude. As a mermaid, our tears are known to have healing powers. So, I asked Skye to collect them in case she ever needed them in the future. She took my tears and wore them around her neck as a reminder of our friendship and alliance. She promised she would never take it off.

Skye interrupted and said, "I have kept my word. I never take it off. I keep my promises."

Amidst the chaos, Skye pulled me aside and confessed that although she loved me, she didn't love me enough to leave her current life behind even after what I told her. She gave me a hug before diving back into the sea to return to Mermaid Island. Gabriel asked Jaserula what did you tell her? Jaserula said that is something to ask Skye. Gabriel turned to look at Skye, who had tears in her eyes, and shook her head no. Jaserula said to Gabriel now you know the story and why I don't trust her.

But now, here we were with Skye's new boyfriend trying to make a deal with me. She offered to give me the trident that had been lost for centuries in exchange for safe passage for her and her crew and current lover. If I agree to her terms, she will hand me the trident. Jaserula snarled, looked at Skye, and asked, "Do you want to meet her"? Skye, still in shock with Jaserula's words, shook her head no. Skye looks at Jaserula and asks, "So, do we have a deal for the Trident for the safe passage of my crew."

Jaserula said, "Yes, we have a deal."

Suddenly, Skye tried to pass off a box containing a horn - one of the treasures that belonged to Jaserula that she had given to her. Jaserula refused it, telling her that she might need it again someday. Secretly, she thanked me for not telling her Gabriel the truth about what she had told her on the day they parted ways. Skye thanked Jaserula, and she and Gabriel made their way back to their row boat.

As they quickly rowed back to their ship, Gabriel couldn't help but notice that Skye had not given Jaserula back the mermaid crown she had found. But before he could say anything, they were already onboard the ship. Skye quickly instructed the crew to leave immediately before Jaserula changed her mind. They sailed away at top speed. Gabriel commented on the missing crown, and Skye simply smiled and said nothing.

Skye stood at the helm of her ship, feeling the wind in her face and a sense of accomplishment for successfully navigating them past Mermaid Island. She glanced back at her crew, all busy with their tasks, and smiled. They had finally obtained the treasure they had been searching for, and now it was time to head home. But as they sailed on, Skye couldn't shake the feeling of unease. She still hadn't made up her mind about Gabriel, the naval officer who had joined their crew on this journey. And now, she was questioning whether he would turn her in for her crimes or return to his duties with the Queen's Navy.

Before she could dwell on these thoughts any longer, Gabriel's hand rested on her arm, bringing her back to reality. "I believe we are finally in safe waters," he said.

Relief washed over Skye as she nodded in agreement. It felt like they had been on a perpetual chase for months, with Admiral Barrack and the Queen's Navy hot on their trail.

But just as Skye began to relax, Patches shouted from below deck. "Admiral Barrack and his ship are closing in on us fast!"

Panic set in as Skye knew they were no match for Barrack's ship - twice their size and heavily armed. She gave the orders to stop the ship and drop anchor, flying the white flag of surrender.

Her crew was shocked, but Skye knew it was the only way to keep them safe. She promised them that they would be free to go once she surrendered herself.

Gabriel stood next to her, his expression grave as he asked what she was doing. She explained her plan and reminded him of their deal - she had given him her word that she would turn herself in. Gabriel said, "That was no longer necessary." Skye said a pirate's word is their bond and never breaks it. Gabriel agreed to what she was doing but didn't like it. He stood by Skye's side as Barrack's ship pulled alongside theirs, and his officers boarded with smirks on their faces. Skye couldn't help but feel a twinge of regret. But she knew it was the only way to end this constant running and bring justice for her crimes. She wanted her crew to be safe.

With a heavy heart, she surrendered herself to Admiral Barrack, knowing that her crew and treasure would be safe in Patches' hands. She could only hope that Gabriel would keep his word and not turn his back on her when they reached land.

Skye marched onto the deck, her sword at her side, ready to defend herself and her crew. But Gabriel stepped in front of her, blocking her path and whispering, "I'll handle this."

He turned to the Barrack ship and spoke to the captain. "We agreed to capture Captain Skye, not her innocent crew. She may be ruthless, but she's the one with the bounty on her head. Her crew fears her - if they step out of line, she slits their throats."

Skye looked at him incredulously, wondering what he was doing. But Gabriel continued, speaking about how the men were terrified of her, some even trying to escape and being captured and tortured by flogging.

"Trust me," Gabriel added, "they are happy to see her go."

Scabbage and Patches chimed in, yelling that they wanted Skye off the ship, too. The admiral looked into Gabriel's eyes and asked if all of this was true. Gabriel nodded solemnly and told him about Skye's greed for treasure - she never shared it with her crew. When the captain asked about their latest failed treasure hunt, Gabriel shook his head sadly. "Someone had already pillaged whatever might have been there at one time." Skye couldn't believe what she was hearing - Gabriel was lying to protect her and her crew. At that moment, she loved him even more. Admiral Barrack thought it over before deciding to only take Captain Skye and leave the rest of the crew alone - they had been through enough. Skye turned on her heel and shouted at them, calling them cowards and threatening to flog them if they didn't follow orders. The crew snarled back at her, shouting insults as she was led away in shackles. While everyone was distracted, Gabriel made a quick trip to Skye's cabin, where he searched through drawers and finally found what he was looking for. He grabbed it and slipped it into his pocket before returning to the Barrack ship.

Gabriel's boots pounded against the wooden deck as he sprinted towards the stern of the ship. He glanced back at the crew, who had become like family to him during their time at sea and silently prayed for their safety. His gaze fell on Chef, who was descending down the stairs out of sight. With a quick salute and a wave, Gabriel hurried on his way, determined not to be left behind.

Upon boarding the ship, he immediately sought out information about where Skye had been taken. A crew member pointed him towards the barracks, and with a heavy heart, Gabriel made his way there. However, he knew it would look suspicious if he went directly to Skye's cell, so instead, he tried to appear nonchalant as he searched for Admiral Barrack and his officers.

After a brief knock on the admiral's cabin door, Gabriel was greeted with an "enter" and stepped inside. The room was spacious, with a separate bedroom and sitting area filled with bottles of wine from all over the world. The walls were adorned with a portrait of the current queen and king, as well as ships in bottles and various knick-knacks collected from around the world. However, what caught Gabriel's attention most was the large collection of weapons displayed proudly in one corner of the room. Each weapon held a story of victory in battle for Admiral Barrack.

As they exchanged greetings, Admiral Barrack praised Gabriel for finally capturing notorious pirate captain Skye. He assured Gabriel that the bounty on her head would make him a wealthy man, able to settle down and start a family. But deep down, Gabriel knew that all he wanted was to be with Skye - no amount of money or status could replace her.

Despite his inner turmoil, Gabriel forced a smile and accepted the drink that was being handed to him by one of the officers. They all raised their glasses in a toast to Gabriel, celebrating his success. As the night wore on and the officers became increasingly drunk, Gabriel discreetly made his way down to the barracks.

He found Skye's cell and fought back tears as he saw her sitting alone, a shadow of her former fierce self. With trembling hands, he reached through the bars and held onto hers. He promised that he would find a way to get her out - he couldn't bear the thought of her spending a lifetime in prison or, worse, being hanged for her crimes.

As they sat there in silence, holding onto each other through the bars. Gabriel knew that their love would persevere through any challenges thrown their way. No amount of wealth or power could ever compare to what he felt for Skye. Gabriel heard a noise behind him and knew the guards were coming to check on their prisoner. Gabriel quickly stepped back. Skye also stepped back.

Skye started pacing back and forth in her cramped, musty cell. Her heart fluttered with both fear and longing. She wanted nothing more than to run into his arms and have him assure her that everything would be alright. But she held back, knowing there were two guards watching her every move.

Gabriel was the first to speak, his voice harsh and accusing. "Finally, the dirty scoundrel is where she belongs," he bellowed. "Your crew is probably celebrating right now, drinking your fine wines and rum."

Skye bristled at his words and retorted, "They better not be, or I'll kill them myself."

Gabriel let out a cruel laugh. "You won't be torturing anyone anymore. Your crew has been set free to go wherever they choose while you sit in this cell awaiting trial before Queen Ava."

Skye couldn't help but shudder at the thought of facing the queen's judgment. Ever since the pirates had kidnapped her sister and killed her in cold blood, Queen Ava had shown no mercy towards them. Some she tortured for days before sentencing them to death; others were simply hung without a second thought. And sometimes, she took pleasure in putting them on display in the village square, where the villagers would throw rotten vegetables at them.

Gabriel stood close to the bars, whispering softly to Skye. "Are you okay?" he asked, knowing they were being watched.

Skye nodded her head slightly, not wanting to show any vulnerability in front of the guards.

"I will speak to Queen Ava on your behalf," Gabriel promised. "We've known each other since we were children. I was the one who delivered the news of Princess Kalieanna's death to her family."

Skye shook her head, resisting his offer. "You don't need to do that for me," she whispered. "I will face the consequences of my actions." But before she could say anything else, Gabriel's demeanor changed. He suddenly snarled, "Stay away from me, you wench! I won't be tempted by your evil ways. You will pay for your crimes!"

With a violent shove, he pushed something through the bars and ran off, leaving Skye alone with her thoughts and a small object in her hand. Skye sat on the hard prison bed. She was surrounded by cold, gray walls and metal bars. As she waited for the guards to leave, she reached under her mattress and pulled out a small cloth napkin. Inside were two stale rolls and pieces of cheese, along with a note from Gabriel encouraging her to be strong.

Meanwhile, in a nearby cabin, Gabriel lay on the bed staring up at the ceiling. He clutched a small item he had taken from Skye's desk, hoping it would hold some clue to help her escape. Despite his exhaustion, he couldn't stop thinking about how to get her out of this situation.

Back on the Vixen, Patches, Scabbage, Eric, Scar, and Chef huddled together, discussing their next move. Patches argued that their orders were to return home and hide their treasure. But Chef reminded them that Skye was their captain and they needed to stand by her. Scabbage became angry and shouted at Patches for blindly following orders instead of fighting for their captain's freedom. But Patches eventually revealed he was just messing with them, and they all laughed in relief.

As they made plans to rescue Skye, she woke up in her cell, realizing this wasn't just a nightmare. Her mind raced with thoughts of breaking out and taking down the guards.

Skye gave her word to Gabriel that she would stand trial, and she was determined to keep her promise. As Gabriel tossed and turned in his bed, he pieced together a plan for Skye's defense, unsure if it would be enough to save her. He couldn't shake the guilt of forcing her into this situation, but he hoped his plan would work. The ship jostled as it docked at the port, and Gabriel hurriedly grabbed the locket he had taken from Skye's desk before making his way to the top deck. He needed to speak with the queen immediately. Gabriel made his way off the ship to seek out Queen Ava and speak on Skye's behalf.

As Skye waited in her cramped cell, she mentally prepared herself for the trial ahead. The thought of facing a queen who despised pirates made her anxious, but she refused to show any weakness. Suddenly, the door burst open, and guards marched in, shackling her wrists and ankles despite her protests. She tried to reason with them, telling them she would go willingly, but they only sneered and yelled insults at her.

Being led onto the deck, Skye was greeted by Admiral Barrack with a smug smirk. He taunted her, claiming that justice would finally be served for all of her crimes. In response, Skye defiantly spat at him, earning a backhand across the face in return. Her lip started swelling, and she could taste blood in her mouth as they continued to drag her off the ship. They arrived at a door that resembled a servant's entrance and made their way through winding corridors lined with paintings of past royals. Eventually, they reached a grand throne room where a regal chair sat at the front. Skye knew this was where she would face judgment for her actions as a pirate.

As Skye was escorted into the courtroom, she couldn't help but feel a sense of dread wash over her. The chair at the front of the room was ornately carved and fit for a queen, which made her heart race even faster. On either side of the room, benches were filled with people who had come to witness her sentencing. The guards prodded her forward, and she walked down the narrow aisle between the crowded faces. They sneered and shouted insults at her - thief, liar, murderer, filthy pirate - their words like daggers piercing her skin. She felt a wave of hissing coming from all directions, and she knew that she was as good as dead. Skye looked in the crowd for Gabriel couldn't find his face anywhere. He was probably afraid to be associated with her; she still felt disappointed he wasn't there.

When they reached the front of the room, an announcement rang out: "Now presenting Queen Ava." As the queen entered and stood before them, everyone in the room bowed except for Skye. The guards tried to make her bow, but she snarled at them, refusing to show any respect to someone who was not her true queen. Queen Ava then instructed everyone to take a seat as she addressed the crowd.

"We are here today to see justice served for the notorious Captain Skye," Queen Ava began. "She is one of the most wanted pirates in all the land, and her fate now rests in my hands."

The queen stepped closer to Skye and circled around her like a predator stalking its prey. She asked Skye the question that would determine her sentence: "How do you plead?"

Before Skye could answer, chaos erupted from the back of the room as her crew burst through the doors. They were shouting and causing a commotion as they tried to reach their captain. Patches' voice boomed above the others as he shouted, "There's our captain!"

Guards quickly moved to block them from reaching Skye, but they continued to yell their support for her - no matter what punishment she received, they would stand by her side. Queen Ava turned to Skye and asked if these were her crew members. Skye shook her head furiously and explained that she had told them to leave her and go home. The queen then signaled for the guards to let them pass.

Skye's crew rushed up to her, hugging her tightly as they celebrated their reunion. There was a lot of commotion in the courtroom, but Queen Ava quickly regained control. Queen asked the crowd to be silent and for Skye's men to control themselves. Skye thought to herself; the Queen does speak with authority and commands attention. She would make a good pirate captain Skye laughed to herself. Queen Ava pulled something out of her pocket - a small locket. Skye's eyes widened in shock as she saw it and shouted, "Locket! How did you get my locket?" She searched the room frantically until she spotted

Gabriel, who had betrayed her. She pointed at him accusingly and yelled, "You thief! That was my personal belonging! How dare you take that!"

The queen interrupted their exchange and turned to Skye. "Where did you get this locket?" she asked sternly, "Did you steal it? And from whom did you steal it?"

Skye took a deep breath and looked directly into Queen Ava's eyes. "I didn't steal it," she stated firmly. "I've always had it. My father gave it to me when he found me - a baby abandoned in an alleyway. He said it was a picture of my real family who either didn't want me or couldn't keep me."

Queen Ava opened the locket and said this is a picture of my mother and father and me and my younger sister. Skye was taken aback and asked, "Why would I have a picture of your family? There must be a mistake".

My father gave that to me. Skye sighed; tears came to her eyes she realized now her father had lied to her. Her father, after all, was a notorious pirate captain. He probably stole it and gave it to her to comfort her.

Skye looked at the Queen and said, "My father gave that to me. I just believed him. He must have stolen it." Skye was about to speak when Chef interrupted her. He took Skye's hands and said, "Your father didn't lie about the locket you always had when he bought you at the auction block; he didn't steal it."

Queen Ava stepped in and asked Chef, "What do you mean by auction block."

Chef explained that pirate captains bid on orphans to come on their ships and work. Queen Ava held up her hands and addressed the crowd. She told the crowd to be silent. A hush fell over the great hall. Queen Ava announced that the court was over and ordered everyone to leave.

Skye noticed a woman in the background who seemed familiar, but she couldn't place where she had seen her before. Suddenly, Gabriel approached the queen and whispered something in her ear, causing her to have a shocked look on her face. Queen Ava asked if Skye promised not to run away when the shackles were removed. Skye nodded in agreement. The Queen ordered the guards to remove the shackles and take Skye to the Blue room to get cleaned up. Skye was led to a room where servants were waiting with a drawn bath and clothes for her to wear. Despite their attempts to help her, Skye insisted on bathing herself and dressing on her own.

After finishing up, she was brought a beautiful sky-blue dress with layers of soft silk material and a tight girdle that made her feel uncomfortable. She couldn't understand why the queen was going through all this trouble just to punish or kill her. Soon enough, there was a knock on the door, and Gabriel entered. In frustration and anger, Skye grabbed anything she could find and threw it at him as she yelled at him to get out.

Gabriel's voice trembled as he pleaded, "Just listen to me." But Skye remained firm, "No, listening to you got me and my crew arrested. You gave the queen my locket, the only thing I have from my biological parents. I have nothing to say to you; just leave." Gabriel left in defeat. A few minutes later, there was a rap on the door. Skye grabbed a nearby vase defensively but was stopped by the maid, who announced that the queen's lady-in-waiting, Gisela, had arrived to escort her to the queen's presence.

Meanwhile, at the queen's sitting room, Chef sat sipping tea with the Queen Mother as they chatted about the day he first met Skye. He couldn't help but notice a painting on the wall that bore a striking resemblance to his captain. Curiosity getting the better of him, he asked the Queen Mother about it. She replied with pride, "That is a painting of my mother, Avanna Kalieanna. The queen was named after her and our second daughter was given her middle name - Kalieanna, who has been missing for over 20 years."

Chef exclaimed in surprise, "She looks just like our captain."

The Queen's mother replied " When I saw her from afar, she reminded me so much of my own mother I was taken back."

The queen entered the room and joined them excitedly. "Do you think it could be her?" she asked eagerly. "After all these years of believing her dead, she was hiding as a pirate?"

Before anyone could respond, there was another knock on the door. A servant opened it to reveal Skye standing outside in a blue frilly dress. The servant announced her as Captain Skye and invited her inside.

The queen welcomed Skye with open arms and thanked her for coming. Skye couldn't resist commenting on the uncomfortable dress she was wearing. Chef spoke up, "You look beautiful! I can't wait to tell the crew; they won't believe me." Skye shot him a glare. The queen ignored her comment and expressed her curiosity about something.

Skye's hands trembled as she sat before the imposing Queen Ava. She couldn't help but notice the delicate china tea set and the embroidered cushions that adorned the room. It was a stark contrast to her own rough, weathered appearance. Skye nervously fidgeted with the lace on the uncomfortable dress she wore as she spoke.

"I'm curious, Your Majesty," she began, "how do you treat all of the pirates you capture?" The queen raised an eyebrow at this unexpected question. "We do not invite them to tea if that's what you're wondering. They are either sent to prison, hung, or flogged depending on their crimes."

Skye couldn't hide her shock. "So you fancy yourself their judge and jury?"

The queen's face remained stern, but Chef interjected, "Skye, please listen to what Her Majesty has to say before making judgments."

Reluctantly, Skye sat down and allowed the queen to pour her a cup of tea. She wondered if this was all a bad nightmare. She took the cup of tea from the Queen. She was in such shock she could barely taste it.

"You should let it cool first," the queen advised, noticing her discomfort. "Or blow on it."

"Right," Skye mumbled, feeling out of place in her frilly dress and sipping tea in a palace.

"What is it you wished to discuss with me?" she finally asked, trying to focus on the reason for her being here.

The queen produced a locket and asked, "What do you know about the origin of this locket?" Skye replied with her usual answer, "My father said it was on me when he found me."

But the queen continued with a surprising story. "This locket belonged to my younger sister, Princess Kalieanna Wilamean Larksen, until today."

Confused, Skye asked, "Why have you changed your mind about her death?"

The queen's expression softened as she looked at Skye. "After seeing you today and hearing what Gabriel has told me, I believe you are my long-lost sister."

Skye gasped in disbelief. "That's crazy! I am a pirate, not a princess. I don't know the first thing about being royalty. You must be mistaken." What did that lying thief Gabriel tell you? He explained that you have the same heart-shaped birthmark my sister has on her upper thigh.

Skye glared at Gabriel and said now you are telling about our sex encounters. Gabriel shook his head and said no just that I had seen it when we went swimming. Now Skye was a bit embarrassed; she just told the Queen that she and Gabriel were sexually involved. Queen Ava smiled and assured her it didn't matter how he saw it. Captain Gabriel is an honorable man with a good reputation. So I took him at his word. Skye replied that a lot of people have birthmarks. How can you be so sure I am her? Skye was getting frustrated and started to get up to leave.

But Chef tapped her on the shoulder and gestured towards a painting hanging on the wall of the queen's grandmother.

"Why do you have a painting of me in your sitting area?" Skye asked, feeling a sense of unease. The queen explained, "It is not you but my grandmother. And you bear a striking resemblance to her."

She then showed Skye the locket with pictures of her parents, King Jakob and Queen Jaslyn, on one side and pictures of herself and another child on the other side.

"You just turned seven, and I was nine," the queen said softly. "You said my mother seemed familiar to you because she is your mother."

Skye's head spun as she looked between the queen's mother, who had tears in her eyes, and Gabriel, who had been silent throughout this revelation. She couldn't deny the similarities in their features and suddenly everything made sense. The familiar feeling she had upon entering the palace, the strange connection she felt with the royal family. Unable to process everything at once, Skye stood up and walked over to the painting, staring at it in disbelief. "Is this some sick joke?"

The queen shook her head solemnly. "It is not a joke, Skye. You are my long-lost sister and the lost princess."

Tears welled up in Skye's eyes as she struggled to come to terms with this new reality. But deep down, she couldn't help but feel a sense of belonging that she had never felt before.

As Skye looked around the queen's chambers, she was overwhelmed by the presence of her mother, her sister, the Queen, and Gabriel. She felt like running away, but where could she go? Instead, she ran out of the chambers and down the hallway. Skye didn't know where she was going; she just needed to get away and think. Her mind was racing as she stumbled into a nearby room filled with toys and stuffed animals. It was a child's bedroom, and as Skye explored it, memories came flooding back to her - playing with her sister Ava, inventing new gadgets, singing lullabies with her mother, and having supper with her family. She remembered growing up in the castle and befriending Gabe at the orphanage before he became a captain.

Overwhelmed by these sudden memories, Skye realized that Gabe was Gabriel after all these years. But where was her father, King Jakob? She couldn't find him anywhere. Lost in thought, Skye didn't even hear the gentle knock on the door until the queen entered. Skye wasn't sure how to react to her long-lost sister but was quickly comforted when Ava opened her arms and welcomed her home.

Tears streaming down their faces, Ava and Skye stood there hugging each other tightly while their mother watched with joyous tears of her own. After 20 years apart, they had so much to say to each other. Skye looked over at her mother and waved her over to join in the hug. The

three of them just stayed there, hugging each other. Gabriel came into the room, seeing the three of them, was filled with emotion himself. The Queen addressed Gabriel and said thank you so much for bringing my sister home to us you can have any reward you wish.

Gabriel refused any reward from Ava. He was just happy to see them reunited at last.

After 20 years, Princess Kalieanna finally returned home to Queen Ava. As they embraced, the queen asked. "Are you okay there, Gabe?". The queen suggested they retire to her chambers, as the guards would worry if they didn't know her whereabouts. She offered warm tea, but Skye requested whiskey or rum instead. Ava laughed and ordered the servants to go get their best whiskey. We are celebrating the return of my sister. Ava wanted to know all about Skye and her life as a pirate captain.

As they sat together in the queen's chambers, Ava couldn't stop smiling at having her sister back. She had so many questions about how Skye became such a wanted pirate and captain of her own ship, but she didn't want to overwhelm her. Eventually, she couldn't contain her curiosity any longer and asked.

The two sisters talked for hours, catching up on each other's lives. It felt so good to be together again. Suddenly, Ava got an idea and announced that they needed to throw a ball in honor of Skye's return home. Though hesitant at first, Skye couldn't resist her sister's excitement and agreed.

Before leaving to find Gabe and her crew, Skye made sure to ask if they could attend the ball as well. Ava happily agreed and even promised to prepare rooms for them and proper attire for them to wear.

As Skye made her way to the study, where she knew she would find Gabe and the rest of the crew, she could already hear their laughter echoing through the halls. When she entered the room, she saw Gabe, Chef, Eric, Scar, Gavay, Patches, and Scabbage all gathered around a table enjoying liquor and food.

She asked where the rest of the crew was, to which Patches replied that he had sent them back to the ship. Skye agreed that it was a good idea, knowing how rowdy they could get.

Feeling content and surrounded by her loved ones, Skye couldn't help but smile as she joined her crew in their celebration. One of the servants came into the study to announce dinner would be at 7. The crew looked at each other, unsure if they were included. The servant could see their hesitation and assured them everyone was invited, the Queen insisted. They all grabbed their drinks and headed to the grand game room.

As Patches and the others entered the grand game room, The room had two billiard tables, dart boards, and card tables. Patches commented it looks like a grand bar. Queen Ava stood at one of the billiard tables with a regal posture. Her dark hair was swept up in an elegant bun, and she wore a deep blue gown adorned with jewels, greeted them warmly, and invited them to sit down.

Ava asked if anyone was up for a game of billiards. Patches couldn't help but make a joke about addressing Skye as "princess," causing Skye to roll her eyes and laugh. Ava asked Skye do you play? Skye said yes. Patches replied whatever you do, don't take her up on any bets. Next thing you know, she will own the castle. Everyone laughed. Ava agreed. Skye racked the balls and told Ava she could go first. The rest of the crew engaged in a card game. Gabriel, always respectful, excused himself to check on their needs and found some of the finest liquor from the queen's collection. Everyone was enjoying themselves. Ava and Skye were laughing and having fun. Ava said to Skye I think you are going easy on me. Skye laughed and said who, me. Skye could have easily beaten Ava but wanted to extend their time together. Skye finally did win and asked if there were any other takers. Her crew all shook their heads no. Chef complained of being hungry and went off to the kitchen. Skye assured him that there was already a kitchen staff in place, but Chef insisted on taking charge. Gabriel followed him to ensure he didn't harm anyone or ruin dinner.

As they settled in and made themselves at home, One of the Queen's servants entered the game room to inform them that their quarters were almost ready. Skye noticed Patches trying to sneak a gold candlestick into his pocket and quietly scolded him before Ava saw. Ava reassured them that there was no need to steal as she would reward them for keeping her sister safe during their journey.

Skye then mentioned that Chef had made his way to the kitchen and promised Ava a delicious meal as thanks for their hospitality. As Ava looked concerned about having an outsider in her kitchen, Skye reminded her that Gabriel was supervising him to make sure everything went smoothly.

As they continued to chat and enjoy each other's company, Ava excused herself to attend to her duties as queen and get ready for the ball she was giving on her sister's return. Skye waved in some hesitant servants who had been waiting outside and asked if their rooms were ready.

Once Ava left, Skye signaled for the men to wrap up their conversation and retire to their rooms to freshen up for dinner. Patches, always the jokester, grabbed a bottle of rum and joked about getting thirsty during the long walk. Skye rolled her eyes but couldn't help but smile at their antics.

As she poured herself a glass of wine and sat down to relax, Skye thought about everything that had happened that day, from waking up on the ship as a prisoner to now being treated like royalty by the queen. It was quite a whirlwind of events, but she couldn't deny that she was grateful for this unexpected turn of events.

Skye slowly blinked her eyes open, and as she did, the memories of her past life came flooding back. She was no longer a prisoner on death row, but instead, she was Princess Kalieanna, long lost daughter of the king and queen. Her childhood friend Gabriel walked into the room and greeted her with a smile. He reminded her that, technically, she should be called Princess Kalieanna, not Skye. But knowing how much she loved to be called "Kal," he teased her about it. She felt a mix of emotions as she thought about reclaiming her true identity after living as Skye for so many years. As they reminisced about their childhood adventures, Gabriel revealed his guilt for involving her in a dangerous mission that ultimately led to her kidnapping and false death. But Skye assured him that she had no regrets and had lived a fulfilling life full of travel and treasure hunting. As they shared a tender moment, Patches interrupted them and laughed and reminded them to save their affection for later when the children weren't around. Everyone laughed at his comment and Skye couldn't help but notice how handsome he looked without all his facial hair.

They were preparing for a ball the following night and tonight was a practice run to work on everyone's manners, including hers. As the rest of her crew arrived - Scabbage, Eric, Chef, Scar, and Gavay - Skye couldn't help but admire how clean and well-dressed they all looked compared to their usual rugged appearances on their pirate ship. Chef nervously assured them that dinner was under control and they could expect multiple courses since they weren't on a ship anymore. Skye poured everyone some wine from a bottle she had chosen herself due to her father's insistence on giving her a well-rounded education. Queen Ava joined them and complemented Skye on her wine selection, revealing that she had also been educated by their father. Skye couldn't help but feel grateful for the family she never knew she had for the family she did have. Skye stood next to Scabbage, dressed in a formal navy blue dress that hugged her curves. Her eyes sparkled as she chatted with the others, sipping on a glass of wine poured by Patches, who seemed to be enjoying their conversation. Skye looked outside of the study to see Gabriel, a woman hugging him, crying I thought I lost you. Skye's chest tightened. She thought, oh no, he did have a wife; she felt heartbroken. Suddenly, Gabriel walked into the study, looking handsome in a dark navy suit. Skye couldn't help but notice how well his suit matched her dress. He complimented her on her beautiful sapphire necklace and asked where she got it. She inquired who that woman hugging you was, was it your wife. Gabriel laughed and told the woman to come over to him and said, "Skye, this is my sister Katie. Do you remember her?" Skye looked at her and smiled, "Of course", and gave her a big hug. Katie asked where she had gotten her necklace. Skye then smiled and told him and Katie about a treasure hunt she went on near Egypt. As they continued chatting, a servant announced that dinner was ready. They made their way to the grand dining room, where the table was long enough to fit fifty people, and there was even a mirror to hold double that number. Skye remembered when they used to eat in a smaller dining room attached to her parents' suite when she was a child. As everyone took their seats at the large table, the queen instructed Skye to sit on her right and the queen mother on her left while the others were free to choose their own seats. Before long, Chef entered wearing his signature white smock and hat, followed by servants carrying trays of food. Everyone's plates were set in front of them, and the silver covers were removed to reveal an exotic dish of snails for Patches, who let out a loud scream at the sight of them. The rest of the guests chuckled as they began their first course of dinner.

The queen's laughter filled the dining hall as she explained to Patches that the small, slimy creatures on his plate were called escargot, a French delicacy. She shared how the chef had saut~ed them in white wine, butter, fresh garlic, and thyme from her own garden. The aroma of the herbs made Skye's mouth water as she watched her sister flirt with Patches, who seemed hesitant at first but was encouraged by the queen to try one. With guidance from the queen, Patches mastered the art of extracting the snail meat and exclaimed how delicious it was. The queen reminded everyone of dinner etiquette, instructing them to wait for her before digging into each course.

"Your Majesty, I have prepared your favorite soup," Chef said, bowing respectfully to the Queen. As the servants cleared their plates, they were replaced with bowls of creamy asparagus soup, the queen's favorite dish.

The Queen smiled graciously, her eyes sparkling with delight as she took in the creamy, parmesan-infused asparagus soup in front of her. "It looks absolutely delicious," she exclaimed before taking a sip.

The chef grinned proudly as the guests sang praises about its flavor and asked about the use of paprika. The queen confirmed that it was one of the secret herbs in the recipe, much to Chef's delight. After savoring every last drop of soup and homemade rolls, everyone eagerly awaited the next course. Skye and Ava sat on one side while Patches and the Queen mother sat on the other.

Meanwhile, Skye leaned over to whisper to Ava, "Are you trying to charm Patches?" Ava blushed and shook her head, but Skye could tell by her coy smile that there was more to it.

After everyone had finished their soup, Chef returned with the main course - stuffed Cornish hen with red baby potatoes and green beans. The smell alone made Skye's stomach rumble with anticipation.

"The rolls are amazing, too. Did you make those as well?" Skye asked the Chef eagerly. "Yes, I did," Chef replied with a proud grin. "But please save room for dessert."

"What did you make for dessert?" inquired Skye.

"A chocolate souffle," announced Chef with a twinkle in his eye.

"I've never seen you make that on the ship," Patches chimed in. "Why not?"

Chef chuckled. "It's not possible with all the noise and movement on the ship. You need a quiet kitchen for the souffle to rise perfectly."

As they finished their main course, the servants cleared their plates and dessert was brought out - individual mini chocolate souffles placed in front of each guest. The rich aroma of warm chocolate filled the room, making everyone's mouths water.

"This is truly divine," praised the Queen, taking a bite of her souffle. "If you ever need a job, Chef, you have one here in my kitchen."

Skye playfully chimed in, "Hey, are you trying to steal our chef?"

Chef laughed and replied, "Ladies, no need to fight over me. I promise to cook for the Queen every time we visit."

Queen Ava's radiant smile illuminated the grand dining room as she gracefully accepted the chef's terms. The table hummed with satisfied chatter as everyone raved about each mouth-watering course, their plates now empty and ready for a post-dinner drink.

As they moved to the ornate study, Patches eagerly followed Queen Ava's suggestion while Gabriel poured drinks for the group. Skye, still reeling from her recent discovery of being a long-lost princess, took a moment to catch her breath in the elegant drawing room surrounded by her newfound family. However, Queen Ava pulled her aside and questioned her plans now that she knew her true identity. Skye hesitated, unsure of what direction her life would take now. Skye wasn't sure if she was cut out to be a princess and do princess duties. Skye enjoyed being a pirate and living on the sea and treasure hunts. She smiled at Ava and said she wasn't sure what her plans were. She thought to herself there is also Gabriel to consider now that he was home with all his memories back. He would probably want to stay here and settle down.

Meanwhile, Gabriel seized the opportunity for some alone time with Skye, expressing how much he missed her since arriving at the castle. A mischievous grin spread across Skye's face as she invited him to join her in her chambers later that evening.

As the night came to a close and everyone retired to their rooms, Skye's maid helped her prepare for bed. As she was settling in, there was a sudden knock on her door. To her surprise, it was Captain Barrack, urgently requesting to speak with her. Skye stood guard at the doorway, not allowing him entry without a valid reason. She noticed

Gabriel discreetly positioned behind a nearby wall - his protective presence offering some comfort.

Captain Barrack revealed troubling news about someone seeking revenge against Skye. Although she couldn't think of anyone who would want to harm her, she promised to be cautious and grateful for the captain's warning. He left with a stern reminder to stay vigilant with so many guests present at the upcoming ball.

As Barrack bid good night to Skye, she could still smell the faint scent of cigarette smoke on his clothes. She shut the door, and a minute later, there was a knock. Expecting it to be Barrack with more information, Skye opened the door to find Gabriel standing there instead. He had all the information Barrack had shared with her earlier, but she had forgotten he was coming by.

Gabriel asked about Barrack's visit, and Skye explained the situation. "I better go and tell the crew," Gabriel said. Skye agreed, but Gabriel suggested they wait until morning since they were probably asleep. But as soon as Gabriel took her into his arms and planted a ravenous kiss on her lips, Skye couldn't resist any longer. They spent the night together ravishing each other until their exhausted bodies finally fell asleep. When the maid woke Skye up in the morning, Gabriel was gone. The maid informed her that her sister Ava had left a message for her to quickly get ready because there were lots of things to do before the ball that night.

Skye put on a beautiful violet dress, feeling unsure if it suited her or not. Looking in the mirror, she barely recognized herself. Just days ago, she was a notorious pirate captain wanted by the law, and now she was dressed like a princess. It was a lot to process. While Skye enjoyed spending time with her sister and mother, she couldn't shake the feeling that her heart belonged to the sea and her life as a pirate. She knew she would have to tell Ava about her decision eventually.

Leaving her room, Skye went to meet up with Ava in the ballroom, where she was busy arranging vases filled with flowers for the event. Ava greeted Skye with a smile but confessed that she was feeling stressed about making everything perfect for their first ball in years. She also mentioned how excited she was to introduce Skye, her long-lost sister who had finally returned. Ava asked Skye if she would be okay with being introduced by her given name, Princess Kalieanna

Wilamean Larsen of Dansk. At that moment, seeing how stressed and excited her sister was, Skye couldn't bring herself to tell her that she wouldn't be staying. So, she agreed to be called by her given name for the ball.

After Ava left to attend to other tasks, Skye saw this as the perfect opportunity to go down to her ship and check in with her crew. She wanted to make sure they were prepared in case anyone was seeking revenge against her. As she was about to leave the castle, Gabriel caught up with her and questioned her actions. Skye explained that she wanted to see her crew and gather information for herself instead of having Scabbage or Eric do it for her. Gabriel then pointed out that if she wanted to blend in, she should probably change out of her princess dress. Agreeing, Skye told him to give her ten minutes before meeting on the front porch. Rushing to her room, Skye asked the maid for help in changing into something more suitable for a pirate captain.

Skye paced back and forth in her room, her mind racing with thoughts about the upcoming ball. She had asked Gabriel to give her ten minutes before they met on the front porch. With the help of her maid, she quickly changed into her favorite pirate pants and a loose shirt. As she made her way outside, Gabriel was already there, holding two horses for them to ride. Skye climbed onto her horse effortlessly and grinned at Gabriel. "Hope you can keep up," she teased. They galloped towards the docks where Skye's beloved ship, filled with her loyal crew, awaited them. The familiar cheers of her crew lifted her spirits as she stepped onto the deck.

But their joy was short-lived as Skye relayed the news Barrack had shared with her the night before - someone she had betrayed was seeking revenge and vowed to make her pay. Her crew scoffed at the idea, knowing how much Barrack disliked Skye, and often tried to rattle her. But still, Skye couldn't shake off the strange feeling in the pit of her stomach. Skye told her crew to scout around and see if they could find anything out if the rumors were true. The crew agreed and said they would report back anything they find out. She also told them there was a big ball tonight in her honor, so they needed to be on guard. She heard an "aye-aye, captain." Skye told them she needed to go back to the castle before she was missed.

As they rode back to the castle, they were greeted by Ava, who scowled at Skye's mismatched outfit. "You can't wear that to the ball!" she exclaimed.

Skye laughed, "I am a pirate, after all."

"Please, Skye," Ava pleaded. "Just this once, can you try to look like a princess?"

Sighing, Skye promised to change and rushed back to her room. To her surprise, on her bed lay a beautiful royal blue ball gown with delicate lace details near the bosom area. The silk material felt soft against her skin as she put it on. Her maid helped style her hair into an elegant bun and placed a stunning diamond tiara adorned with sapphires on top of her head.

Looking at herself in the mirror, Skye couldn't help but feel like a princess. But her thoughts were interrupted by a knock on the door - it was one of the queen's servants, requesting her presence in her sister's chambers before the ball.

Skye made her way to her sister's chambers and was let in by one of the servants. She saw her sister wearing a gorgeous yellow sunflower dress, matching necklace, and crown. It was still strange for Skye to see her sister as queen, but she couldn't deny that she looked regal and elegant.

As they chatted, Skye couldn't help but feel grateful for her sister's love and support. Despite their differences, they had each other's backs, and that was all that mattered. As they made their way to the ballroom together, Skye couldn't shake off the feeling that something was about to happen. She reminded herself to stay alert and be prepared for anything as she entered the grand room filled with unfamiliar faces. Ava stood next to Skye, her dress shimmering with gold and silver threads as she handed her a small box. Inside was a stunning necklace featuring diamonds and royal blue sapphires. "It matches your dress perfectly," Ava said with a smile as she fastened it around Skye's neck.

"Thank you," Skye said, admiring the necklace in the mirror. She finally felt like a true princess. Their mother entered the room and gasped at how beautiful Skye looked. "Kalieanna, you look stunning," she exclaimed, using Skye's full princess name.

Mother announced that it was time to enter the ballroom together. She took each of their arms, and they walked down the grand staircase to the awaiting guests.

The queen mother made her grand entrance first, followed by Skye, who heard her new name being announced - "Princess Kalieanna Wilamean Skye Larson." She couldn't help but smile at the addition of her birth name.

Finally, Queen Ava made her entrance, commanding respect and admiration from everyone in the room.

As they mingled with their guests, Skye was about to head over to the feast when Gabriel approached her. "Let me accompany you to the feast, your Highness," he said with a kind smile. Skye accepted his offer, and they stood together eating the delicious food when her mother signaled that it was time for the first dance. As they danced across the floor, Gabriel asked if she knew how to dance. Skye confidently responded that she had learned from Patches, an excellent dancer who was currently dancing with the queen.

Soon, others joined in on the dance floor and it was filled with flowing gowns and twirling couples. Skye couldn't believe this was all happening to her - she truly felt like a princess.

As Skye twirled around the ballroom with Gabriel, Queen Ava caught her attention and signaled for her to join them on the dance floor. The three of them danced gracefully until more guests joined in and filled up the dance floor. After a while, Skye's throat felt dry and she mentioned to Gabriel that she could use a refreshment, preferably a nice cold ale. He smiled and gallantly offered to get one for her. When he returned with the drink, Skye couldn't help but comment on how fast he was. "If it's for royalty, we don't wait," he joked. Skye couldn't help but think she could get used to this kind of treatment.

The ball was in full swing as music played, delicious food was served, and everyone seemed to be having a wonderful time. Queen Ava was making her rounds to greet all the guests and introduce Skye to them. Eventually, they came across King Durank from Holland. He greeted them both with a gracious bow and introduced himself. As they continued walking, Queen Ava asked Skye how she was finding the event so far. Skye replied that everyone seemed very nice, but there were so many people with different names and titles that it was hard to remember them all. Queen Ava reassured her that it takes practice and she would eventually get the hang of it.

Suddenly, there was a commotion at the back of the ballroom as two guards burst in, shouting for the queen's immediate attention. Queen Ava and Skye made their way to the door while asking the guards to step outside for privacy. Both guards seemed visibly upset as they explained what had happened during their nightly rounds. They noticed something strange about the vault door - it wasn't fully closed - so they went inside to check and found that all of the gold coins, crowns, and jewelry were missing. The queen immediately demanded to be taken to the vault, and the guards obliged. Before they left, one of the guards mentioned that there was a note left behind. The guard handed Skye a folded paper with a familiar crest on it. As she opened it, her eyes widened in shock. It was a letter addressed to her from someone named Shayella, claiming to be her daughter. Ava and Gabriel overheard the conversation and were equally surprised by this revelation. Skye took a deep breath and began to explain.

She told them about Jaserula, a mermaid she had been intimate with seven years ago. Skye didn't know at the time that mermaids could mate with both males and females and become pregnant. When Jaserula told her she was pregnant and wanted Skye to go with her and become a mermaid, Skye refused and said hurtful things in the heat of the moment. She didn't believe Jasola and thought she was just trying to manipulate her into leaving her human life behind. However, as time passed, Skye realized how wrong she had been and regretted her actions deeply.

She turned to Gabriel and said that she was surprised Jaserula never mentioned this to him when they reunited. Skye explained that in their last encounter, Jaserula had said some hurtful things to her before swimming away, leading Skye to believe that she was lying about being pregnant. But now, looking back on it all, Skye felt immense guilt for how she treated Jaserula and their unborn child.

Skye looked at Ava and Gabriel with tears in her eyes and promised to make things right. She would do whatever it takes to find Shayella and make amends for her past mistakes. And until then, she assured Ava that she had plenty of treasure on her ship to support the kingdom until they could recover their missing coins.

Gabriel gently placed his hands in hers, fingers intertwining with hers. Skye's eyes were filled with tears as she remembered how much she had missed him and how scared she was to tell him what had happened. "I'm sure you did the best for your daughter, raising her in the safety of the sea with Jaserula," he said softly.

Ava watched their reunion, a mix of emotions flickering across her face. She couldn't help but feel sorry for Skye, knowing that she had missed out on so much of her daughter's life. "How could I have been so blind?" Skye thought to herself, feeling guilt gnawing at her conscience. But Ava wasn't done yet. "That still doesn't explain how your seven-year-old daughter managed to orchestrate such an elaborate scheme," she interjected, her voice sharp with accusation. Skye took a deep breath before explaining. "You see, mermaids live for centuries, but their growth is rapid when they are born to keep them safe from predators. Once they reach adulthood, their aging slows down drastically. So technically, my daughter is already twenty-one years old."

Ava's jaw dropped in shock at this revelation. "That's...a lot to take in," she stuttered.

"You mean I have a twenty-one-year-old daughter who schemed against me and stole your treasures?" Ava asked incredulously.

"Yes," Skye replied grimly. "And I need to go after her right away."

Ava immediately offered to come along and help, but Skye declined. "No, you need to stay here and run your country. Keep up appearances so no one knows anything is wrong."

As if on cue, Patches and Scabbage entered the vault at that moment. Skye quickly gave them instructions to retrieve her gold coins discreetly from the ship and bring them to the vault. "We need to set sail immediately," she added. "We have a thief to catch."

Ava held Skye's hands tightly and promised, "I trust you'll find my treasures and return them to me."

In a gesture of trust, Ava handed her royal ring to Skye and said, "If you get into any trouble, show this to anyone who questions your actions. They'll know you're on a mission for the queen." She then asked her servant to fetch some paper, a quill, and her seal.

"I'll write a letter declaring that you are working as an agent for me," Ava explained. "That should help explain any unusual behavior."

Meanwhile, Scabbage, Scar, Eric, and Patches returned with large treasure boxes filled with gold coins. Ava was amazed at the amount of treasure before her and exclaimed, "No wonder you were on the most wanted list!"

Skye smiled proudly at her crew. "When they heard that their queen was in trouble, they all chipped in their own treasures to help," she explained. "They've been such loyal and gracious companions on our journey."

Patches chimed in, "And we got our captain out of being hanged because of it."

Ava was touched by their selfless actions but also felt guilty for not keeping her treasures safe. "You didn't have to do this," she insisted.

"Yes, we did," Patches replied firmly. "We feel responsible for not protecting your treasure better."

Skye couldn't be prouder of her crew at that moment. "Double the guard duty and get a better lock," she instructed them.

But Patches already had a solution in hand. He pulled out some chains and a large lock from his pocket and proclaimed, "Already taken care of, captain."

The servant returned with a piece of parchment, a quill, and the queen's royal seal. Ava hastily wrote a pardon for Skye, clearing her of all charges and allowing her to work for the royal navy. As she handed the document to Skye, tears streamed down her cheeks. "I just got you back," Ava said, her voice choked with emotion. "Now I'm losing you again." Skye took her hands and promised, "I'll come back to you." She then asked a servant about the whereabouts of the queen mother, who was currently at a ball trying to assure guests that everything was under control. Skye urged Ava to go back to the ball and act as if nothing had happened, explaining that there was an emergency on her home island that she needed to attend to immediately. After saying their goodbyes and hugging each other tightly, Skye turned to her crew and joked about them not giving all of their gold to Ava. Patches assured her that they hadn't even touched her secret stash, much to Skye's relief.

As they prepared to leave, Skye searched for Gabriel, knowing it would be difficult to say goodbye to him. Suddenly, Chef entered and offered his sympathies for the news. He explained that he had stayed behind with the queen mother to avoid causing any commotion at the ball. When Skye asked if he had seen Gabriel, Chef shook his head no. Just then, the queen mother appeared and engulfed Skye in a tight hug, tears streaming down her own face. In a quiet voice, she expressed how much she loved and missed her daughter before reminding her to be careful on her journey.

Despite searching desperately for Gabriel, there was still no sign of him when it was time for them to leave. As they made their way towards the exit, Skye finally spotted Gabriel. Stewart suddenly appeared in the doorway with a knife in hand. Skye immediately knew his intentions - he was going after Gabriel. She screamed a warning to him, causing him to stop and turn just in time for Stewart to thrust the knife into his side.

As Stewart laughed, he revealed that Jaserula had sent her regards. He attempted to flee, but Patches and Scabbage quickly apprehended him. Meanwhile, Skye rushed to Gabriel's side, blood gushing from his wound. She frantically searched for a way to save him, knowing she didn't have time to retrieve the precious Sapphire stone from their ship.

Tears streaming down her face, Skye begged Gabriel not to die. In a weak voice, he responded that he didn't have much time left. "I wanted to tell you something," he managed to say before slipping away. Skye collapsed beside him, heartbroken and filled with regret that she never got a chance to hear his words.

Tears streamed down Skye's face as she desperately searched the vault for anything that might help. Gabriel, lying on the ground and barely conscious, whispered her name. She knelt by him, and he weakly stated that he didn't have much time left. With a trembling voice, he professed his eternal love for her. Skye felt guilt wash over her as she apologized for dragging him into this dangerous mission. But Gabriel only smiled, saying every minute spent with her was worth it. Suddenly, he took his last breath, and Skye became hysterical, trying to wake him up and pleading for him not to leave her. Ava, who had been watching from afar, tried to console Skye but was pushed away. As Skye's glass vial necklace swung back and forth, Chef ran over and suggested using mermaid tears to save Gabriel. Skye quickly opened the vial and poured the liquid into Gabriel's mouth, praying it wasn't too late. For a moment, everyone around them held their breath as if nothing seemed to happen. Tears streamed down Ava's face as she resigned herself to Gabriel's death. But then, a faint whisper of Skye's name caught their attention. They watched in amazement as Gabriel slowly sat up and declared that he felt fine, just a little light-headed. Skye checked his wound and found it completely healed, thanks to the powerful mermaid tears. Patches exclaimed at their strength while Skye held onto Gabriel tightly, relieved that he was alive. Scabbage suggested they continue their mission and catch Shayella before it was too late, but Skye insisted that Gabriel stay behind with her sister for protection. I need someone that I can trust to protect her. Gabriel argued that he would be more helpful on the mission. The queen has her guards. Skye insisted you need to stay; you almost died. I can't bear it if something happens to you again. Gabriel argued I am a grown man, and I am perfectly capable of taking care of myself. Skye shook her head and said no. This angered Gabriel, who, without saying a word, stormed off.

Skye's heavy dress rustled as she made her way down the narrow hallways of the ship, trying to find her cabin. She regretted wearing it and couldn't wait to change into her usual pirate attire.

As she passed by the crew quarters, she shouted orders for them to prepare to depart immediately. Skye was a little annoyed with Gabriel for not even saying goodbye before they left port. But she had bigger things to worry about right now.

In her cabin, Skye struggled to undo the tight laces of her dress, cursing under her breath. She could feel the ship moving as they sailed away from the dock. Skye groaned at the thought of having to ask someone else to help her with the laces but then remembered she had a knife on her belt. With a quick slash, she freed herself from the frilly dress and changed into her trusty black silk pants and fitted white top.

Feeling more like herself again, Skye grabbed her sword and bag before heading up on deck. She wanted to check in with Chef and make sure he had enough rations for the crew. As she approached the galley, she heard Chef's voice and someone else talking inside. She walked in to find Gabriel there, helping Chef prepare meals.

Surprised to see him, Skye asked if he was hiding a stowaway in his kitchen. Chef explained that Gabriel wanted to come along and help them out, much to Skye's annoyance. But when Gabriel mentioned that Ava insisted he come along to keep Skye safe, she couldn't argue. After all, Ava was their queen.

With a shake of her head, Skye agreed that they needed all the help they could get. She filled Gabriel in on their mission: finding Shayella using clues left behind on a note. Skye laughed at how much Gabriel enjoyed solving puzzles. After studying the note a little more, Skye exclaimed I know where she is going. She pointed to the symbols around the note she was going after heart shape ruby. It is supposed to be able to stop time. She is headed to Dragon's Island. It is said that the Heart Shape Ruby is hidden there, and it can stop time. We cannot let Shayella get her hands on that Ruby and imagine the damage she could do. It is believed that Dragons live on the island and protect the Ruby. Gabriel looked at her and said now you are telling me there are living Dragons. Skye shook her head and said yes. Skye told Gabriel and Chef she needed to go up on deck and give the crew their new heading.

Before heading up on deck, Skye took a moment to appreciate the fresh sea air and the feeling of being back in her element. She was glad to have her sister and mother back, and deep down, she was also glad that Gabriel had sneaked aboard. She didn't know what dangers they would face on this journey, but at least they would face them together. She gave her crew the new coordinates and new destination, Dragon's Island. Some of the crew members had a look of concern on her face. Skye ignored them and headed to the helm.

To Be Continued

Epilogue

Evil Shayella, half-mermaid and half-human, has stolen all of Queen Ava's treasure as revenge against Captain Skye. Shayella left a note with clues about where she had taken the treasure. From the clues on the note, Skye and her crew have determined that Shayella is after the Red Ruby Heart Stone, rumored to have the power to stop time. Legend has it that the Ruby Stone is hidden on Dragon Island, protected by the oldest dragon, Draco, who despises humans. Now, Captain Skye is on her way to Dragon Island to recover her sister Queen Ava's treasure and stop Shayella from retrieving the Red Ruby Heart Stone. If Shayella gets her hands on that stone, there's no telling how much damage she could do. Hopefully, Captain Skye and her crew will get there in time.

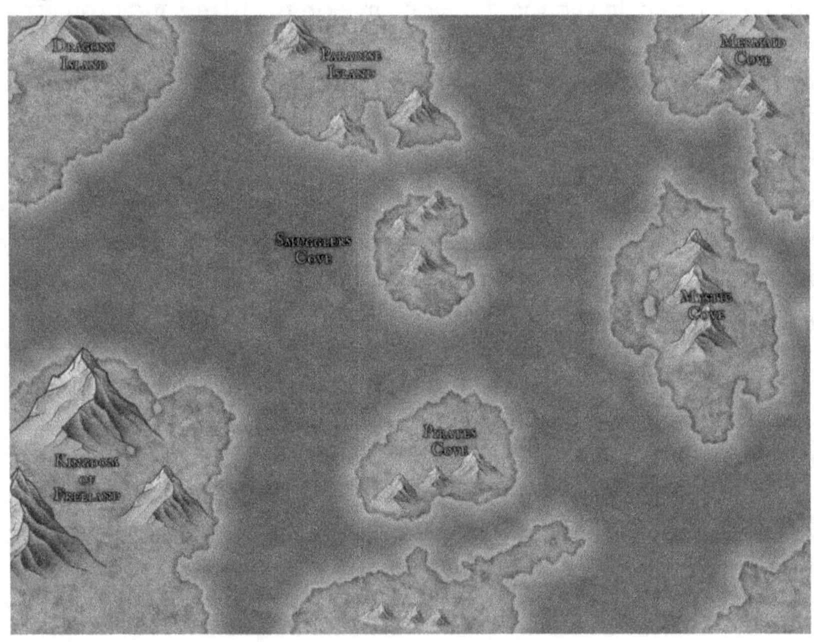